Quickies /kwi-kk-eez/

1. Noun (or maybe not) :
   a short fight wherein the hero shows off his abs more than beating up the villain.

   - ✓ Inspector Abhay Pandey had indulged in various *quickies* that had won him a few medals and promotions (not to forget a whole lot of girlfriends).

2. Verb :
   a shot of eye-candy or tonic that gives instant energy.

   - ✓ Daroga ji scanned her long legs and rounded bottom for a *quickie*. What would he not do for a quickie behind the same door that she had held open for him.

*Don't bother about the meaning of the word, just sit back and let **Daring Daroga** take over.*

Other Quickies you can pick:

Dark Temptation: The Naughty Proposal!
Two strangers meet and kindle desires long repressed. Then they meet again and explore some more. Without the shackles of a relationship binding them down, they indulge in sinful pleasures, amorous games and unbridled passion. Will they end up in love? Or are they in for a surprise?

Criminal Masterminds: Catch Me? No You Can't!
Raja Tiwari is freshly out of jail, and not just because of stealing hearts and killing with his looks. He is looking for a new job, and lands up in one, topped with a silky bonus.

With ex-cop Thakur, and the sexy Silky Sinha, he has to pull a task that could make him rich or land him back behind bars. Will he play his angle and beat everyone else to the end?

*10 Rules of F**g Around*
Ronnie Singh believes in the age-old adage - practice makes a man perfect - and he believes in practicing every day. With different partners. Or multiple partners.

While beer and hash form his staple diet, hooking up with a different chic is the prime motive of his life. An expert in this art, he has a few rules, which applied correctly can get him the girl of his dreams. Will his rules help him mount the pinnacle?

DARING DAROGA

Killer in the Shadows!

Amit Nangia

Quickies

SRISHTI PUBLISHERS & DISTRIBUTORS
N-16, C. R. Park
New Delhi 110 019
editorial@srishtipublishers.com

First published in Quickies by
Srishti Publishers & Distributors in 2015

10 9 8 7 6 5 4 3 2 1

Text copyright © Amit Nangia, 2015
Series copyright © Srishti Publishers & Distributors, 2015

The author asserts the moral right to be identified as the author of this work. All characters in this book are fictitious, and any resemblance to real persons, living or dead, is purely coincidental.

Disclaimer: The songs used herein are solely for entertainment purpose and reflect no other interests. While due care has been taken to give credit to copyright holders of the same, any omission is deeply regretted and shall be corrected in future editions. Song credits: pp. 1, 5: *Dabangg* (2010), T-Series; pp. 43, 44: *Bodyguard* (2011), T-Series; p. 69: *Wanted* (2009), T-Series; p. 98: *Jai Ho* (2014), Eros; p. 105: *Gangs of Wasseypur* (2012), Eagle Home Entertainment; p. 105: *Shootout at Lokhandwala* (2007), T-Series; p. 108: *Apna Sapna Money Money* (2006), Tips Industries Limited.

Police Constable Shukla shivered and stamped his feet as the wind rolled an empty beer can across the cobbled road. He checked his watch: ten minutes past seven. He wondered when inspector *sahib* would come, wishing him to come soon. He had far better things to do tonight than stand guard over a dead body.

Shukla pulled out a wad of chewing tobacco, rubbed some on his hand and stuffed it into his mouth. Above his head hung an enamel sign, the wrought-iron resembling a strangled body, creaking as it swung in the wind. The faded sign read *Sulabh Shochalaya*, with an arrow pointing downwards.

Shukla was still adjusting the tobacco in the folds of his lower lip when he heard the sound of a car approaching with a music system so loud, it seemed like a DJ playing at some wedding. "*Hud hud dabbangg dabbangg*" blared from the speakers. He almost danced two steps as he spit his tobacco aiming at the beer can. His aim was very good – not with the gun, but with the tobacco spit.

Headlights flared as a mud-splattered, dark green Mahindra Jeep rumbled over the stones, coming to an uncertain halt. To Shukla's dismay, the music stopped. The door opened and a handsome man wearing a tailored, crisp police uniform hugging the bulging shoulders, broad chest and firmly shaped abs stepped out. With his glossy

1

black hair, and an equally crisp red scarf round his neck, he looked more like a Bollywood hero than a policeman.

Shukla immediately stiffened to attention, but was waved at ease.

The wind found the beer can again and dribbled it across to the inspector, who gave a mighty kick and sent it flying through the air past Shukla's ear, to rattle and bounce down the toilet steps.

Shukla grinned and swung his torch beam toward the depths. "Shall we go in, sir?"

"What's the hurry to enter a toilet, Shuklaji? If he's dead, he'll wait for us. Besides, I've got my new uniform stitched today for Billo Rani and I don't want to mess it up sooner than I have to."

It was the *Chhamia* party tonight. Police Inspector Abhay Pandey had prevented yet another bank robbery and every victory was celebrated with female dancers *(chhamia)*, booze and tandoori chicken.

Inspector Abhay fished a battered packet from his trouser pocket and brought out a cigarette. "Shuklaji, what the hell were you doing here at this hour?"

Shukla gulped in his tobacco. "*Sirji kya karein, control hee nahi hua.* Loose motions, that too in superfast motion, sirji."

"*Kya baat kartey ho Shuklaji.* I don't need the details of your shitting patterns. Tell me about the dead body. And speed it up. The alcohol at the party is going to run out before you reach the punch line."

Taking the hint, Shukla speeded up his narrative, "As you know, sir, these toilets have an attendant only till 6.00 p.m."

"I didn't know," grunted Abhay. "I always pee in shop doorways."

"Anyway, sir," continued Shukla doggedly, "I thought I'd better investigate."

Abhay snorted. "Investigate what? Illegal peeing after 7.00 p.m.?"

"Not much more to tell, sirji. I went inside and found this man sprawled on the floor. He looked dead. And Dr. Nanda lives round the corner only, so I went and brought him here."

"What did the quack say? "Abhay fiddled with his cigarette box.

"He found bloody knees and a damaged spinal cord. He said death was caused by a strong blow on the base of the skull. He has called the post-mortem team anyway and they should be here any moment."

"I suppose we can't put the evil moment off." Abhay pinched out his cigarette and stuffed the butt back into the packet. "Let's get inside before people think you're trying to pick me up for the night."

One hand gripping the iron handrail, he followed Shukla's torch cautiously. The echoing, monotonous plopping sound of dripping water grew louder.

"Flaming hell, Shukla, it's awash down here. You might have bloody warned me."

"It wasn't as bad as this before, I promise sirji," said Shukla. "One of the tanks is overflowing and the body's blocking the drain."

"This gets better and better," the inspector observed bitterly. "So where is he?"

Shukla swung his torch and illuminated a drenched shape huddled in one corner. "I'm afraid we're going to have to get our feet wet, sir."

As they stepped in, the water found holes in Shukla's shoes he never knew existed. The heap in the corner looked like a mess of wet rags, but the torchlight revealed it to be a man. A dead man. He lay on his back in the flooded urinal stalls; his long, matted hair bobbling in the rising water; wide-open, sightless eyes staring unflinchingly into the burning glare of the torch. The mouth was agape and dribbling, the beard and ragged overcoat filthy with vomit that stank of stale, cheap alcohol. The body of a man who had crawled into some dark corner to die.

"Heroin!" exclaimed Shukla, his torch beam slowly creeping over the emaciated figure's arms, highlighting needle marks. "That's an expensive habit."

"Well, by the look of him," observed Abhay, "I doubt if he wasted money on nonessentials like soap and food." He prodded the body with his foot, and then turned away. A match flared as he relit the butt. "I suppose you haven't been through his pockets?"

"Not yet," the constable admitted.

"This is basic investigation you need to do," Abhay replied grimly adjusting his scarf. "And you would have done it, constable, had you spent more time on your job and less on looking for whores in the dark lanes."

In the dark, Shukla blushed. He believed his womanizing was a well-kept secret, but nothing seemed to escape the seemingly unobservant Inspector Abhay Pandey.

"*Sirji, woh baat nahin hain na.* He's a bit messy, so I didn't feel like checking him."

"Well, he's not going to get any bloody cleaner floating in pee, is he? Can we quickly finish this investigation as the water is rising here? It's up to my ankles. I feel like a traveller on the *Titanic*."

Shukla bent down, and checked the dead man's pockets. He found a photograph and a bundle of cash neatly placed in an envelope. He handed both to Abhay.

Abhay looked at the photograph and kept looking. She was young, but not too young, maybe in her late twenties and quite a looker. Dark hair, rich, creamy flesh, and the most sensuous mouth Abhay had ever seen. His thoughts about the woman got interrupted as Shukla's nose came in between his view of the photograph. Shukla was ogling over the photograph like a dog with his tongue out when he sees a bone.

"Shuklaji!" Abhay shouted. "Why are you staring at the photo? *Pahley kabhi ladki ki photu nahin dekhi kya?"*

"*Sirji, woh baat nahin hain na.* I have seen a lot of photographs, but *yeh to bilkul maal hai sirji."* Shukla grinned.

A smile returned on Abhay's face. "*Kya baat kartey ho Shuklaji,* your honesty is what I like."

Abhay looked at the photograph again, capturing the girl's face in his memory. "*Vaisey hai toh bilkul maal.*" Shukla's giggles were muffled by the sound of an approaching vehicle: the postmortem team had arrived. Two people took a stretcher towards the public convenience.

Abhay kept the cash and handed the photograph to Shukla and said, "Run a check for this photograph."

"Sirji, what about the cash?"

"What cash? We never found any cash; this is the fund for the next *chhamiya* party." Abhay smiled as they entered his jeep. Abhay started the ignition and the music started:

Arrey mann balwaan, lagey chattaan, rahey humesha aagey; Hud hud dabbangg dabbangg dabbangg dabbangg...

Shukla smiled and started head-banging like a rockstar. He loved this song. Abhay pressed the accelerator, eager to reach the party where Billo Rani's dance performance was waiting for him.

Abhay got a call on the radio while he was still on his way. He lowered the stereo's volume and watched Shukla still dancing.

"Inspector Abhay Pandey here," he said.

Abhay turned to Shukla and said, "Intruder. Possibly a murder case. House 501, Meerapur. Only thing she said was, 'Help me, I think I've killed somebody.' Then she must have passed out or..."

Abhay knew what that meant. She might be hurt, she might be dead. Or the whole thing might be nothing. As a policeman, he never knew what he was going to walk in on, but ironically, he always had to be prepared for anything.

"We'll be there in five. Over," Abhay said.

Abhay glanced at his constable. Shukla was still enjoying the music as if nothing had happened. He used his tongue to lick the tobacco paste coming out of his mouth. The man was disgusting.

Shukla looked up to see his boss watching him with disapproval. He shook his head in frustration and said through a mouthful of tobacco, "*Sirji, aaj chhamia party mein humara jaana mushkil lag raha hai.* All hell is breaking loose in this town today only. This is the sixth call we've had. What does a guy need to do to get to a decent victory party without someone dying?"

Abhay knew how 'decent' their victory parties were. He smirked at Shukla's honesty. Even he wanted to be in Rani's arms tonight. *"Kya baat kartey ho Shuklaji, duty bhi toh zaroori hai.* Let's just quickly finish this and then we can go to the party." He flicked on the police siren and drove to the crime scene.

"I just hope this isn't the same crazy woman who has been calling almost every day at the station,' said Shukla increasing the volume of the car stereo.

Abhay kept his eyes fixed ahead as he weaved his way through the traffic, ignoring Shukla's nonchalant attitude. Abhay loved the fact that most of the cars slowed down or quickly got out of the way to let the police car with a siren pass. In fact, he used this siren most of the times to avoid traffic, even if he wasn't going to any crime scene. He swerved the jeep into the parking lot in front of the house, and as he got out of the car, Abhay's hand automatically checked for his gun.

Both of them walked up silently to house number 501. It was shrouded in darkness, and the front door was unlocked.

Shukla swallowed in some air, "Sirji, this looks like a *bhoot bangla.* I have heard some ghost stories around this place too."

"If you don't stop blabbering, I will make you a ghost. Concentrate on the case!" Abhay said, as he placed his cold gun on Shukla's forehead.

"Yes, sirji. Full concentrate. Let's go!" Shukla entered the house first, his flashlight leading the way, its dim beam of light sweeping the room. Abhay followed him, his alert eyes piercing the darkness and scanning the area. He studied the house. A simple beige leather sofa set faced an LCD unit. The room was sleek and neat. Unlike most women's houses, it lacked pink fluffy pillows and tons of knickknacks and embroidered stuff. A few unpacked boxes had been pushed into a corner. The walls were white coloured and there were no photographs of family or friends anywhere. That seemed odd. There was a small collection of novels stacked on a table and an assortment of some law related books on a wooden book shelf.

Sofa, chairs, LCD TV – all fairly normal but empty. Shukla checked the small white kitchen, flicked a pizza piece lying on the slab and gave Abhay the all-clear nod. Abhay opened another door which he found was the bathroom. Small but neat. He made a mental note that the front living area hadn't been disturbed. Just then, they heard a faint moan somewhere in the back of the house.

Hiding behind the kitchen wall, Shukla gulped the whole pizza slice in one go and then came out and looked at Abhay. On his order, they tiptoed their way to the door from where the sound seemed to have come. Abhay eased the door gently, his gun ready. A thin ray of moonlight sliced the darkness and fell on a figure lying in the creased bed. There was broken glass shattered on the floor, and pillows and magazines scattered around. Another groan rang through the air. Abhay remembered Billo Rani's groans from his last encounter in her bed. He moved closer to the figure.

"If there was an intruder, he's not here, sirji," said Shukla.

Abhay stood beside the bed, assessing the situation. The woman groaned in pain. It wasn't an orgasmic groan as Abhay had wished it to be. She was covered in blood and was clutching a bloody knife. Blood oozed from a wound in her right wrist and a tiny droplet marked her throat. "Get me some towels from the bathroom," he ordered Shukla.

Abhay replaced his gun in its holster, took out the knife from her fingers using his crisp white handkerchief, pulled out a plastic bag from his pocket and dropped the knife inside. Shukla went inside the bathroom, spent some time looking at the mirror and admiring himself, moving his hands on his beard. He saw some perfumes lying on the washbasin shelf. He picked and tried a few on him until he heard Abhay shouting from outside. He rushed back with the towels. Abhay bent down and knelt beside the bed and wrapped one towel around her wrist tightly to stop the bleeding.

"Is she going to make it?" Shukla asked, as he watched Abhay wipe the blood off her neck and face.

"Yeah, but she's lost some blood." He looked at the woman and noticed that she was a familiar face. He had seen her somewhere. Oh yes, she was the same girl from the photograph they had retrieved from the dead body a while ago. She had ivory skin and her long dark hair framed it beautifully. She certainly looked stunning in that low-cut black night dress. Too damn low-cut perhaps. He'd noticed the way Shukla had eyed her and sniggered suggestively to him.

"Madam...madam ji, can you hear me?" he asked, gently shaking her.

"*Sirji yeh toh wohi maal hai...hai na?*" Shukla said with a chuckle.

Abhay glared at Shukla and barked, "Moron! Every situation is not good for a joke. Hit the lights and bring the team in to start looking for clues."

Shukla frowned but left the room.

The woman's dark eyelashes fluttered and her soft pink lips trembled as she tried to speak. She had a small frame, which was lost in the blood-splattered black night gown she was wearing. He quickly checked her body to see if there were other wounds. Her skin was flawless, her legs long and slim. There didn't appear to be any other cuts, except a point on her throat which looked like a knife prick. Abhay didn't know how much time had elapsed before he heard the wail of the ambulance siren. A sigh of relief went through him. She was too beautiful to die.

"I killed him..." She mumbled as she regained consciousness. She kicked at the tangled bedcovers in an attempt to escape the horrible nightmare.

She felt a hand grip her arm, and she screamed.

"Sshhhh madam, it's okay. *Hum hain* Inspector Abhay Pandey and you are safe now."

Abhay stared at her inviting cleavage. She drew back and tightened the sheet to her chest. Trembling, she forced herself to open her eyes, expecting to see the person who had tried to kill her. She started to push her tangled hair away from her face, but realized that her fingers were covered in a red sticky substance. Blood. Her stomach churned. Visions of the attack flashed through her mind.

The inspector wiped her palms with a towel. Actually he wanted to wipe her whole body with a wet towel again and again. She certainly was a seductive piece. Her low-cut black night gown revealed acres of warm, creamy flesh just crying out for exploration.

Abhay twisted the scarf around his neck. "Can you tell me your name?"

She nodded numbly. "Naina...Sinha."

Naina kaash tum hoti meri maina, Abhay thought. He offered a smile and said gently, "Just stay right where you are, Naina. The team is going to take you to the hospital. You'll be just fine. Later you can tell me what happened here and give your statement."

It vaguely worried him, but there was probably a logical explanation which could wait, whereas the party couldn't. Naina listened to the man's deep, husky voice calm her. Finally someone was going to listen to her.

Shukla popped in. "Sirji, actually I wanted to say, can we go to the victory party now?"

Abhay gazed stiffly around the police station; it was in shambles.

"This office is a mess, Mishraji. Disgusting!"

"We were just about to tidy it up, sirji," lied Mishra, the head constable, as he removed the dog-eared stack of files from the chair, looked for somewhere to put them, then decided his own table was the only free space. He offered the chair to Inspector Pandey who declined it with a disdainful sniff.

"And how is the party going? They seem to be enjoying themselves," Abhay shouted over the noise. "Not too loud for you, is it?"

"No, sir," lied Mishra as he pushed the phone to his ears. He was the head constable of the police station. A forty-five-year-old man, he had a belly so huge that he wouldn't have seen his own feet since years. He was the backbone of the station. He had spent most of his time behind a typewriter or the phone, than in the field.

"Nice to hear people enjoying themselves...for a change," Mishra said.

Abhay nodded his approval, his gaze wandering around the dingy lobby with its stark wooden benches and the Wanted poster flapping on the dark grey walls. "I never realized just how dreary this lobby looked, Mishraji. Do you think you could see about cheering it up...get in some house plants, or flowers, or something?"

"Yes, sir. Very good idea, sirji," mumbled Mishra, raising his eyes to the ceiling in mute appeal. Bloody flowers indeed! He was a policeman, not a bloody landscape gardener.

Abhay started moving up the stairs to the terrace where the party was going on. He paused and looked back, "Sorry I had to put you on duty tonight Mishraji, but there are very few men I could really trust to do a good job."

Mishra gave a noncommittal grunt and Abhay walked on. He pushed open the door to the terrace letting a warm burst of happy sound roll down the stairs on an air current of alcohol.

The full gang of police officers was dancing around two girls and the music was blaring at full volume. Seeing Abhay, everyone froze, the music stopped. Abhay stepped inside with a stern look on his face, Shukla right behind. All eyes were on Inspector Abhay Pandey; he stuck two fingers in his mouth and ripped out an ear-piercing whistle.

"*Ruk kyun gaye, bajao music!*"

There were yells of delight and a salvo of wolf whistles, and the party started again.

Two uniformed men came in with a wooden charpoy and placed it for the *daroga babu*. One more man came running with a stool and another with a *hukka*. The whole setup was ready in a fraction of seconds. Abhay Pandey untied his scarf from the neck and tied it on his hand as he sat on the wooden charpoy.

Shukla shouted for Abhay's favourite alcohol. "*Sahab ke liye special narangi lao!*"

And then, the sizzler was served: hot Billo Rani's sizzling hot *mujra.*

Her tight-fitting dress did more than hug her figure. It intimately explored it, and they were treated to a glorious display of wriggling buttock cleft as she moved her bums to the music. It looked like some girl had accidentally entered a boys hostel and everyone was drooling over her. The entire police force looked like salivating toads in front of this beautiful woman.

Her magnetic moves charmed the pants of the entire police force, especially that of Abhay. She smiled seductively at Abhay. His intense grey eyes disturbed her, like he could see through her even with her clothes on. But she was enjoying it, as he was the one who'd paid for tonight. With every move, with every touch of Rani, Abhay could feel his junior becoming senior.

Upstairs, the party was throbbing away louder than ever and showed no signs of breaking up. Mishra was sitting at his desk, hearing the stamping, shrieking, roars of laughter, and the sound of glass smashing. A load of bloody hooligans, he thought as he tried to hear what the caller was saying. "I'm sorry, sir. A bit of a disturbance outside. Would you mind repeating that?"

The man on the phone sounded out of breath and was barely whispering into the phone. *"Sirji, meri bhains....* someone stole my buffalo."

As Mishra was writing down the important complaints coming in from the people of the town, he saw Inspector Abhay Pandey and Billo Rani walking downstairs. The inspector and Rani went away in his jeep, and Mishra sneaked upstairs to enjoy the party. He had been eagerly waiting for Abhay's departure. He went upstairs and grabbed a Patiala peg and raised it to the team. *"Abhay ji* gone, *toh hamari* party on. *"*

As they entered a motel room, Abhay locked the room and sat on one of the chairs in the room.

"Strip for me."

The way he said it sounded more like a command than a request. Rani was more than willing to obey as she wanted to earn some good money.

Being with Abhay alone was worse than being in the middle of a group; it was too intimate. His eyes followed her every movement, touching every bare inch of her body. She slowly unbuttoned her costume, feeling the heat of her body rise. She shimmied out of the *ghagra choli* seductively, because Abhay's senior was waiting impatiently.

Abhay slipped an arm around her waist. He kissed her shoulder as he fiddled with the clasp of her bra. Rani sighed and leaned back against his chest. "Oh, yes," she felt him relax, as if he'd been waiting for her. His thumbs brushed her nipples, causing bolts of desire to shoot through her.

"I need to touch you all over, Rani." He turned to face her and slid the bra from her body and dropped it on the floor. She lay down on the mattress, her gaze never leaving Abhay, who slowly began to strip for her. He bared his body without hesitation. His hard muscles and the sexy smile he directed at her made Rani ache. When he loomed naked before her, she quivered in anticipation.

Abhay kissed the sensitive inside of her knee, then grazed his tongue up her thigh. His hot breath caressed her intimate core as he moved up towards her belly. He dropped a soft kiss just below her belly button, while his hands massaged her stomach and thighs. Her hips rose in response; she grabbed Abhay by the arm and made him lie down.

She said hello to senior. Her lips stretched around it, her eyes closed, her expression dazed as she was about to give him the best blowjob he had known in his life. His hands clenched around the strands of hair he held captive, holding her in place, watching her glistening mouth take him. Her lips came down on him in a kiss that sizzled Abhay from his head to his toes.

"You do too many things right." He tried to laugh, but it sounded more like a strained groan. Abhay's breathing turned rapid as his body responded to her mouth. His desire, hot and primitive, grew to a fevered pitch, pulling cries of pure pleasure from deep inside him.

He pulled her back on the bed and slowly climbed on top of her.

She stretched beneath him, flashing a sexy smile. "Hope you enjoyed the moment." Her legs circled his waist.

But Abhay was in no mood to answer. He wasn't answerable to anyone. He wanted more.

He settled between her thighs, pushing himself inside her. He began to move inside her, slowly.

"Too slow. You're torturing me," Rani moaned after a few moments. She clutched his butt, trying to keep him deep inside her.

Abhay groaned. "It'll be my way and it is better this way." He continued his slow movements, all the while repeatedly flickering the tip of his tongue against each of her nipples.

The leisurely pace was driving Rani insane. She pushed up against him, begging him to put out the fire raging inside her body. "I can't take it anymore, Abhay."

His hands tightened on her hips, his muscles tightening as she watched through eyes half closed. His control was strong; dominating her. She tightened her muscles on him again, straining to force him deeper as everything inside her wanted him. His lips were at her neck, caressing her flesh, hard male growls of pleasure echoing in her ears as he shuddered over her. He pressed kisses to her shoulder, his tongue stroking her flesh. She was gasping, begging, distantly amazed that the cries and pleas were coming from her own throat.

He grabbed her wrists and held them captive on either side of her. Tightening his grip, and with a gleam in his eye, he thrust into her – hard and fast, over and over, until their bodies exploded in a mind-blowing climax.

Abhay woke with a jolt and opened his eyes to blazing sunlight. He sat up in bed and snatched up the alarm clock, staring in disbelief – 11.30 a.m. *Oh teri, lag gayi!* The alarm was supposed to ring at eight. He had to see Naina at nine-thirty. He cursed the alarm clock, looked at Rani lying next to him. Junior looked tempted to get senior and go for another round, but he really needed to go.

He broke all speed records dragging on his clothes, which were in a heap on the floor. Then he stopped, sat on the bed, and lit up one of his cigarettes. *What the hell!* There was no point hurrying. If he skipped a shave, skipped breakfast, and roared nonstop to the hospital, he would still be nearly three hours late.

So why not be four hours late? He had a leisurely wash and shave, followed by breakfast. Another hour later, whistling happily, he bounced some cash from the *chhamiya* fund on the side table for Rani who was still asleep, and slipped out. He zipped through the empty roads with his sirens roaring as if he had to reach some crime scene.

He phoned Shukla on the way to the City Hospital and asked him to reach there immediately. Once there, he walked past the hospital hallway enquiring about Naina's room. He smiled to a tall nurse on the way. He loved long-legged women and this nurse had been giving him hints for too long.

Perhaps that was all she needed, because she called out to the handsome *daroga*, "Inspector Sahab, I want to report a crime that happened in our hostel last night."

Abhay was all ears to her story; he loved the attention. *"Bolo, bolo!"*

"It was horrible. I was changing clothes in the nurses' hostel and a trespasser saw me naked last night," said the tall nurse. "He had these awful red, staring eyes ... and his mouth was all drooling."

Who would not, thought Abhay.

The little nurse was all excited with the attention and started off again. "I'd taken everything off... everything... when I realized I hadn't drawn the curtains. I went to the window, and there he was."

Abhay had seen very few nurses who were attractive and she was one of them. He made a mental note to spend some more time with her, sometime soon.

A couple of other nurses and ward boys had gathered around, and a thrill of excitement ran through her audience. "I screamed," she went on. "I thought he was trying to get in, and I was terrified. But hearing my scream, he ran away."

Abhay leaned forward and patted her warm, quivering young arm. "Don't worry, dear. We'll get him."

A pointed cough of disapproval from a doctor passing by made the nurse snatch her hand away hurriedly. Abhay glared at the doctor as he walked past. Then he remembered what he had come in for. He enquired about the way to Naina's ward and reached there thinking about the nurse.

Lying on the bed, she was understandably nervous, and of course worried. But there was something else, something almost secretive about her.

"Hope you are feeling better now and can tell me exactly what happened," the inspector said as he walked towards Naina and propped a pillow behind her.

Naina stared at the handsome man with kind eyes who was asking her these questions. Even in his crumpled uniform, he was looking really handsome.

"You said on the police helpline that you'd killed somebody." Inspector Abhay Pandey stretched one long leg out in front of him. Last night's hangover and exhaustion was kicking in.

"What?" Naina swallowed. She didn't remember making the phone call. She especially didn't remember admitting to murder.

"Was someone in your house?" Abhay stretched his arms and controlled a yawn as he asked.

"I don't understand. He...he had fallen by my bed. Did you not find him? He tried to choke me with a pillow. I couldn't breathe. I fought him, knocked the knife out of his hand. But the room was dark and I tried to call for help, but then everything went dark..."

"Well, we didn't find anybody in your house but we did find a guy in a public convenience near your house. He was found dead and he had your photograph with him. Whatever that may be, you're safe now, Naina," the deep voice said gently. "Try to relax."

Panic crawled through her. "He attacked me. He was going to kill me. What happened to him?" Her breathing was ragged. "W...where is he?"

Abhay was so tired he couldn't even raise a scowl in protest. *Bas kar meri maa!* he thought. *Oh teri, maa sey yaad aaya!* Last night, he had forgotten to inform his mother that he wouldn't come home in the night. *Lag gayi.*

He made a mental note to buy something nice for his mother on his way home. After all, she was all he had. After his father's death in an accident, his mother had raised him up. He had seen his mother live in misery, cleaning other people's utensils and houses and had promised himself that he would give her all the comforts of the world.

He tried to concentrate on the task at hand. His mind was running slow, thanks to the *narangi* hangover and the crime fighting he did all night in the motel room. As he turned back, he heard the door to the hospital room open and close. Shukla was trying to sneak in unseen.

"So kind of you to grace us with your presence," Abhay said, sarcastically.

Constable Shukla entered the room and rattled off, "So sorry, sirji. *Woh kal raat thodi zyaada ho gayi thi.*"

"This hung-over bearded guy is Constable Shukla and he will tell you the details of the investigation," Abhay said to Naina.

The man rubbed his hand over his beard. "Sirji, the team didn't find any clues of an intruder in Naina's house. There seems to be no sign of a break-in. Even the post-mortem report of the man who died before peeing in the public toilet has come in and it states that he died due to a knockout wound on the head, not by a knife." He stared at Naina.

This bearded ugly man didn't believe her. She had dealt with skepticism all her life. His glowering look said everything. Coming back to her hometown had been a mistake. Her grandmother had always told her to stay away, but then she had died and Naina had unfinished business here. She glanced at the constable; he must have recognized her name from when she had called in before.

He probably thought she was a psycho. Naina forced back a sob and tried to think of an explanation, aware that the inspector was studying her. "There has to be a body. He fell right in front of me." But then she'd collapsed, too. Her head still ached and her mind was engulfed in a pall of fog.

"I'll ask you some questions and the naughty man with the nasty beard will write it all down." Abhay had added this for Shukla's benefit as the constable's notebook looked suspiciously devoid of any notes.

With a quick glance to make sure Shukla was recording the details, Abhay then asked, "This knife...is it yours?" He took out the knife from a plastic bag.

Naina nodded. "It...it looks like the one from my kitchen."

"Can you give me a description of the intruder?" Abhay's steady and husky voice mellowed Naina's nervousness slightly.

"I didn't see his face. He was just...strong," she said tugging the sheet tighter around herself. She suddenly realized she was wearing just a skimpy hospital gown and felt a little embarrassed.

"Think, Naina. You might have seen something that could help us. Did he say anything?"

Naina shook her head, realizing how little she had really seen. Instead, she noticed the inspector's strong, carved jaw and the red scarf around his neck. She forced herself to try to remember details about the other man. "He had a mask or something on his face. And he wasn't quite as tall as you."

Shukla scribbled in his small notepad.

Abhay smiled at her. "If you remember anything else, just let me know." He dug around in his pocket until he found a dog-eared card, which he handed to Naina.

"I will," Naina said, tightening her fingers around the bed sheet as she held the card.

Shukla snorted with a glare on his face. "Madam, are you sure you weren't entertaining some guy and things just...well, got a little out of hand?" Shukla asked Naina, his eyebrows raised suggestively.

Anger stirred through Naina. "How dare you imply such a thing! I thought you were supposed to help and protect citizens." She squared her shoulders and tried to sit up.

"You have to believe me," she said, panic lacing her voice. "There was someone there. He tried to kill me." She covered her face with her hands as the memory flashed through her mind.

Inspector Pandey patted her shoulder in a comforting gesture. "Relax, it's over now."

Shukla wasn't so kind. "Ms Sinha, were you drinking last night? Because we found a glass that had alcohol in it and an open vodka bottle."

Naina hesitated. She knew where this line of questioning was headed, and she didn't like it. Not one bit. "I had a glass of vodka," Naina said through clenched teeth.

Shukla then pulled up a bottle of Alprax pills and held it up in front of her. "And these? Did you take some before you went to sleep?"

"I...I've had trouble sleeping. The doctor prescribed them. But I didn't take one last night."

"We're checking for fingerprints. You said you fought him. Do you think you injured him?"

"I...I thought I stabbed him in his arm, but I'm not sure."

Abhay looked at Naina, his thoughts running crazy. He wanted to get inside the hospital bed right next to Naina. Even after last night's ordeal, junior was nearly becoming senior on seeing Naina lying on the bed. To divert his mind, he lit a cigarette.

"We'll have the blood sample from the knife analyzed. It could have been a robbery attempt."

Shukla cleared his throat. "Umm Sirji, there's something you ought to know..."

Abhay shot Shukla a look of warning. "Later Shukla. Right now, we have a crime scene to investigate."

Shukla sighed and left the room.

"I've been getting blank calls," Naina said, hoping to tell her side of things before Shukla took his chance again. "And I've been hearing noises as if someone's been hanging around outside my house. I told the police about it, but they haven't done anything."

"I'll look into it," Abhay said as he kept staring into her beautiful eyes. Even in a hospital gown, she looked so sexy to him.

"Thank you, inspector," said Naina twisting her fingers together as she forced herself to meet his intense gaze.

Abhay's grey eyes grew a shade darker. Naina's entire body tingled with awareness. He could help her. She had to make him believe her. She wasn't crazy. The reporters and people who knew of her background would disagree, but she knew otherwise.

She'd actually lived an active, professional life for the past few years in Mumbai as a successful divorce lawyer. Then she'd moved back to Allahabad, and strange things had started to happen. She'd been a frightened and withdrawn little girl when she'd left Allahabad. But she wasn't a little girl anymore. And she was tired of running away from things.

"Do you want me to call someone from your family to take care of you? Or would you rather go to a friend's house?" Abhay questioned.

"I don't have any friends here," Naina said as she walked towards the couch. She thought of Uncle Chauhan, her parents' friend who lived only a few kilometres away. She hadn't been around him much while she was growing up, but he'd always sent birthday cards and called regularly. And he was her last link to her parents. He had been their best friend. He was also a very rich man, probably one of the richest in Allahabad, and he cared for her deeply. She wouldn't mind being with him at the moment because he had a wonderful way of cheering her up. But she didn't want to bother him with her troubles. Instead, she thought she ought to tell the inspector a little bit about her past before he heard the distorted version from someone else.

"Inspector, you've been so kind. It'll help if you knew a bit about me. I was born here. My parents died when I was a child, so I moved to Mumbai with my grandmother."

"What brought you back to Allahabad?" Abhay asked.

"After my grandmother died, I didn't have any real ties to Mumbai. Also I was tired of the hustle bustle of city life. I am a divorce lawyer and I thought I could continue my practice here."

The truth was that she had to come back. Back in Mumbai, things with her boyfriend Ashish hadn't gone too well. He had started getting obsessed about her. And she needed her space. Uncle Chauhan wanted to see her, and it seemed like everything had come together at once.

After a few minutes, the curtains jerked open and a small doctor emerged, followed by a nurse. The nurse whispered something to the doctor and pointed to the two police officers. He examined them with tired eyes, and then walked over.

"I don't like people smoking in the hospital," the doctor grunted.

"That's all right," beamed Abhay, the cigarette waggling in his mouth. "I don't like people jabbering away while I'm smoking, but I put up with it." There was a burst of laughter by Shukla.

Grinning broadly, Abhay puffed away at his cigarette, making as much smoke as possible. Something about Naina tugged at him. Maybe it was those enormous dark eyes. Or those high, sculpted cheekbones. Or the jet black hair that framed her lovely face like reams of silk.

Abhay rose from the chair and left as the doctor took his place next to Naina. Outside, Shukla was waiting for him. Catching sight of the inspector bearing down on him, Shukla quickly whispered something to a nurse, making her blush, then in a loud voice, said, "Don't forget to call me." She hurried off, giving an apologetic smile to Abhay as she passed.

"Stay away from him, love," Abhay called after her. "He meets men in toilets after dark."

"Sirji," Shukla said, "I don't think anyone tried to kill this psycho."

Abhay gritted his teeth. *"Kya baat kartey ho Shuklaji.* You shouldn't call her a psycho. *Kitni pyari ladki hai."*

"Sirji, don't you know who she is?"

Abhay bit the inside of his cheek to stop himself from cursing Shukla. "Is she a famous model? Miss Allahabad or Miss India, because she really looks like one."

"Sirji, woh baat nahin hain na. We've gotten a couple of calls from her before."

"Yes, she told me that. So why didn't someone follow up on it?"

Shukla grumbled in noticeable disgust. "Two weeks ago, she said someone was prowling outside her house."

"And?"

"It turned out to be a stray pussy. I told you, she's a total nut case, sirji."

Abhay smiled.

"Sirji C A T, cat. Not the kind of stray pussy you are thinking about." Shukla grinned at his remark.

"Shut up, Shukla. There could have been someone there," Abhay frowned.

"She called again last week, saying that someone had been in her office."

"Oh, and what did you find?" Abhay arched an eyebrow.

"Nobody. Sirji, I have seen many such cases. My guess is, she made it all up."

"Shut up, you pussy. Her injuries look pretty damned real to me."

"Well, she's weird. Everyone who grew up around here knows about her."

"And why is that?" Abhay asked, growing tired of Shukla's pussy-and-mouse game.

"Because of what happened to her parents many years ago."

Abhay leaned against the wall. "What about her parents?"

Shukla pulled out a wad of chewing tobacco, rubbed some on his hand and stuffed it into his mouth. "That's the interesting part, sirji. Naina Sinha grew up around here, but she moved to Mumbai to live with her grandmother. Her parents died right here in this town in the same house. As per police records, the father killed the mother and then killed himself."

Abhay swallowed, feeling the cold bite of chill all the way down to his toes. He loosened the scarf around his neck. Through the glass window, he saw the doctor helping Naina. She looked pale and fragile.

"They say Naina witnessed the whole thing, but she doesn't remember it," Shukla continued.

A drop of sweat rolled down Abhay's neck. "How old was she when it happened?"

"Six," Shukla paused, "There's more. The reporters went nuts over the story. The girl had to see a psychiatrist." Shukla spat a blob of reddish brown tobacco juice. "It seems to me like she still may be crazy. There were rumours that she might even have killed her parents. She was holding the murder weapon when the police arrived, and it was a knife from her kitchen. Kind of like the one she had last night. And she kept muttering that it was her fault. Some people say her grandmother whisked her away to cover it up."

A sigh of frustration escaped Abhay.

Naina and the doctor came to the door. She seemed vulnerable and troubled and she'd called him for help. He wanted to protect her. But what exactly was he protecting her from? From some killer or from herself? She could be telling the truth. But if Shukla was right and Naina was unstable, perhaps she hadn't been attacked at all. He wanted to believe her, but he had to check the whole story first. And knowing about Naina's past shed a whole different light on the situation.

Naina brushed her straight black trousers and smoothened her peach silk shirt over her bandaged arm. As she walked into her office, a yawn escaped her. She hadn't felt like getting out of bed because she had barely gotten any sleep. She'd tossed and turned in the bed, wondering who or why someone would attack her. But work was her salvation. Even though she'd always been a failure with people, especially men, she was a whiz at divorce cases – a skill and service her clients paid prime money for.

"Ms Sinha, Devender Singh is waiting for you in your office," Ria, her office assistant chirped. She looked marvellous; she had even polished her face full of make-up and her skin glowed. Her hair was pulled back in a ponytail, and she wore a crisp black formal skirt and a black nylon jacket over a white cotton top.

"He's on the rampage this morning," she added.

Naina smiled. "I expect him to be. He not only received my client's divorce papers, but he just learned he owes her a long list of things and a huge sum of money."

Ria sipped her tea. "You want me to dial 100 if he starts shouting like a maniac?"

"You think we will get some real help on dialing 100!" Naina said mockingly. "Ideally his lawyer should be speaking to me but I think I can handle him."

"Well, good luck with him," Ria said, turning back to the computer.

Naina mumbled a thank you, squared her shoulders, reminded herself of the assertiveness training classes she'd taken in Mumbai and waited for the roaring.

A short, arrogant individual wearing an expensive-looking camel-coloured overcoat, peered distastefully towards her. Devender Singh offered her a mechanical greeting as she entered.

She'd disliked the man the moment she'd met him. He reminded her of the villainous characters Shakti Kapoor used to play in Hindi movies. Short and stooped, he had tiny, red-rimmed, deepset eyes; his face was greasy and black and grey with stubble. His nose, large and route-mapped with tiny red veins, cried out for the urgent attention of a handkerchief. Matted hair flopped over the large collar of the overcoat, which had been made for someone much bigger. He was the Chief Manager at the State Bank of Allahabad, but everyone believed that he had accumulated a lot of money through wrong routes.

"Hi, Mr Singh. What brings you here today?"

Perched on the red leather chair near her desk, Devender Singh looked positively in a rotten mood. He didn't mince his words when he spoke. "You have no right to screw up my life. You are the reason for my divorce. And now you want me to pay such a huge amount."

The anger in his baritone jostled her already taut nerves. But she refused to show it. Instead, she met his anger with a confident smile. "Mr Singh, I am only your wife's lawyer. It was she who feels that you are an ass and decided to divorce you. I'm sorry it worked out like this, but I am just doing my job." She said emotionlessly while fiddling with a pencil.

Singh's cheeks ballooned with anger. Furiously, Singh snatched the pencil from her hand and hurled it to the floor. Pushing his face to within an inch of hers, he said, "You know this will cost me a lot of money."

Naina could smell whiskey on him and it was only 9 a.m. *Bewda kahin ka! No wonder his wife wants to divorce him*, she thought. But Naina refused to let him faze her. "I am a good attorney, and I'm also honest to my clients. Your wife will get what she is entitled to and I will ensure that she does. I am not going to cheat my conscience."

A vein bulged in Singh's pale forehead. "Sometimes, Ms Sinha, you have to look beyond your job. There are worse things than can happen to you. Remember, I know where you live. *Dekh lunga tujhe.*" He threatened her as he picked up his briefcase and left.

Naina exhaled a shaky breath at his implied threat. Could it have been him who had attacked her the night before? The phone rang with a sharp trill that made her jump. Forcing herself to steady her voice, she picked up the receiver.

"Naina, my dear, this is Uncle Chauhan. How are you?"

Naina relaxed, grateful for the familiar voice. She'd missed talking with him lately. "Uncle Chauhan, how nice it is to hear from you! I'm fine. I just got rid of a nasty client, but tell me how you are."

Pradeep Chauhan laughed. His voice sounded shaky, and Naina realized that age had crept up on him while she had been away. "I am good, now that you're back. Well, tomorrow night, we're having a reception in honour of my son Girish, and I want you to be there."

"What's the occasion?" Naina asked. Although she didn't remember Girish very well, Uncle Chauhan had kept her abreast of his son's political activities through his mails and phone calls.

What the mails didn't say was that Girish Chauhan was trouble. Big trouble. He was the son of Pradeep Chauhan, who had been the member of Parliament for the longest time. He had money and he had influence, owning businesses as diverse as security organisations, newspapers, and commercial radio stations. He constantly criticised the police in his newspapers, and was known to be a permanent alcoholic. A rich spoiled brat.

"It's a kickoff for his campaign," Uncle Chauhan said, the pride evident in his voice.

"Like father like son, huh?" Naina quickly prompted.

Uncle Chauhan laughed. "Yes, yes, quite like that! He is filed for candidature for the next Lok Sabha elections."

"Wow," said Naina. "What time is the party?"

"Seven o'clock."

"Sounds great! I'll be there," Naina said. She was tempted to tell her uncle about the incident, but she didn't want to ruin his moment.

Later that afternoon, there was a light knock on Naina's door and Ria poked her head in. She was like the cuckoo bird hiding in a clock. At scheduled intervals, she would peep out and then go back inside the clock. "There's a package for you."

Naina squinted in confusion at the brightly wrapped package. "For me?" Who could be sending her a present, she mused.

"Maybe it's from a secret admirer," Ria said with a wink before slipping out of the door.

Naina removed the small card and read it silently. "Something to remember me by. See you soon."

It had to be from Ashish. But what did he mean he would see her soon? She'd told him she wanted her time and space. *Chaep kahin ka!* For heaven's sake, she'd moved to Allahabad to get away from him. Gingerly, she fingered the delicate baby pink bow and pulled it open. The pale red paper came away easily. A small tape recorder lay in the box.

She pulled it out and pressed the Play button. "*So ja rajkumari, so ja.*"A familiar song started to play. A song that took Naina back to her past. Her mother used to sing a lullaby to this tune when she was a child. A chill slithered up her spine. Her hands shook so violently that the tape recorder fell onto the desk with a thud. The song droned on. Naina covered her ears to drown out the sound. She could almost imagine her mother's soft voice singing the words.

Inspector Abhay Pandey stood in the open doorway of Naina's office, one hand gripping the shiny doorknob, the other fiddling with his red scarf, stupefied as he watched what was going on in front of him. He closed the distance between himself and Naina in a few quick strides.

"I didn't mean to do it," Naina spoke so quietly that Abhay had to lean forward to take in what she was saying.

He didn't have a clue what she meant or even if she knew what she was saying, but he needed to snap her out of this delusional state.

"Ms Sinha," he said, gently nudging her shoulder, "Ms Sinha, can you hear me?"

A childlike cry escaped her. Although he told himself this was strictly business, that this woman might be psychotic, his heart wrenched seeing her like this. All he could see was a sad little girl who was lost and alone.

Ria also heard Naina's cry and came into the room. She was shocked to see the otherwise composed Naina in this state. "I'll get some water," she said and scurried off.

"What...how long have you been standing there?" Naina said. Her voice was weak and distant.

"Not long," Abhay replayed the details of her file in his head. The lack of evidence from the night before complicated things even more. The knife had shown only one blood type and that too of Naina. He needed more information from Naina. "We need to talk."

Ria rushed in and bent down to hand over the glass to Naina, she gave him a bird's-eye view of a deep, inviting cleavage.

"Who sent you this box?" Abhay paid attention to Naina instead.

"I don't know," Naina said in a listless voice.

Abhay turned to Ria. "What did the messenger look like? Was it a courier service?"

Ria bit her lip. "I...I didn't see who it was. I went to the restroom and found it on my desk when I returned."

"*Kya baat karti ho Ria*. You should take your work more seriously." Abhay shook his head observing Ria's small legs. He preferred long-legged women, but could definitely try new genres in life. After all, she had other body parts than just her legs. She had dark, shiny, well-brushed hair, a scrubbed, glowing face, a snub nose, and a broad grin, and yes, nicely shaped breasts.

"I take good care of my work and I can actually take care of anyone really well." She smiled at him. The sort of smile that crept under his pants and gently stroked him.

"Why don't you go home, Naina?" Ria suggested.

Naina nodded.

"Can we go someplace to talk?" Abhay asked.

Naina's dark eyebrows arched in surprise.

"About your case," Abhay clarified. "We need to discuss what we found at your house."

Naina nodded and grabbed her purse. "Okay. Let's go to the cafe around the corner."

Ria opened the door and moved back slightly for them to squeeze past. It was a tight squeeze and she didn't seem to want to make it any easier. Abhay winked at her kind gesture. He could have had a quickie with Ria behind the same door if he had the time to play his cards right.

Abhay followed Naina out. He couldn't help but notice the way Naina's curvaceous backside swayed in her tight black trousers as she disappeared out of the door. The woman definitely had a figure and gorgeous long legs. She pretended like she had all the confidence in the world. But he knew her bravado was a sham. When he'd witnessed her fear only moments earlier, he'd had to order himself not to wrap her in his arms and comfort her. Just the thought made him excited. But a personal entanglement with this woman would be a mistake. Business, buddy, strictly business, he reminded himself as he followed her. Maybe if he told himself that often enough, he would believe it. *Damn!*

Did he know who'd broken into her house? Had he come here to ask her to go to the police station to identify her attacker? A part of her desperately wanted that to happen, while another part of her wasn't quite ready to face the truth. She couldn't remember who'd killed her parents because she couldn't face the truth. That was what the psychiatrist had told her grandmother. Was the truth that horrible for her to accept even now that she was all grown up?

Her stomach turned as the waiter placed cups of tea in front of them. Naina fiddled with the brooch that was pinned on her jacket merely to have something to do with her hands. Taking a deep breath, she looked the inspector square in the eye.

Abhay lit a cigarette. "Ms. Sinha, I think I will call you Naina. Ms Sinha is too formal for me."

Naina nodded.

Abhay stretched out his long legs, brushing his knee against hers. Naina felt a thrill run up her entire body with his touch. She'd been too frightened the night before to notice this man's powerful masculinity. His broad shoulders and muscular body filled out his uniform shirt to perfection. He had a hard, chiselled face with high cheekbones and a red scarf hugging his neck, and dark black hair that looked so thick that she wanted to run her fingers through it.

"You look better now," he said with a slight smile. He wanted to say, *"Mast lag rahi ho"* but he figured that comment would be better understood by Rani, not Naina.

"Thanks. I feel a little better." Naina shifted uneasily in her seat. The way his deep, husky voice murmured her name...it was too personal. And his dark eyes gazed at her in such a way that she wanted to confide in him, to tell him the whole, sordid truth. But if she did, would he still help her?

"Okay, Inspector Abhay Pandey, what did you want to discuss?" Always get to the point, Naina had learned. Take charge of the meeting. Don't let the other person intimidate you.

The inspector was watching puffs of cigarette smoke drift like clouds across the ceiling. His mouth curved into a smile as if he knew exactly what she was doing. She shifted again, this time accidently brushing her leg against his. The soft fabric of his khakis felt warm against her thigh. He smiled again. He wanted to feel her body without the khaki coming in between. Junior felt uncomfortable at the thought.

"Inspector?" She raised her cup for another sip of her tea.

His gaze followed the movement, then suddenly, as if he realized what he was doing, he straightened up in his chair and assumed a more business-like pose. His smile faded, and a serious expression darkened his eyes. "Like I said, the police finished combing your place."

"And?" Naina's pulse jumped.

"They didn't find anything to indicate an intruder."

Naina's hands tightened around the cup. "What about the blood on the knife?"

The inspector hurled out his cigarette, then leaned forward and sipped his tea, and set his cup down with a thud. There was no way of tarting up the facts in fancy clothes. "The tests aren't finished yet but there weren't any other fingerprints except yours, of course." He paused, waiting for her reaction. "If someone was there, they wiped their prints and blood off the knife after you passed out."

Naina leaned back and closed her eyes momentarily. Could she have imagined the whole thing? As a child, she had such vivid nightmares that she swore were real. Could it be happening all over again?

"You want to tell me about the tape recorder? Why did it set you off like that?"

Naina decided that she might as well tell him as much of the truth as possible. "My mother used to sing me that song before she died."

Abhay rubbed his thumb over his scarf. "I can understand how that would upset you. But you don't know who sent it?"

Naina shook her head. "How would I know! You are the police, you should know."

"Maybe someone in the family?"

"I don't have any family. I'm sure you've discovered that by now," she said, her hands tightening around the cup.

Abhay's brief nod told her all she needed to know. Of course he'd read her history. Was he here just to satisfy his curiosity or did he really want to help her?

"No one knew about it except my grandmother." Naina sighed. "And my grandmother is dead now."

"Did she leave you anything valuable? Money, property, jewellery?"

"Why do you ask?" Naina wrinkled her forehead in thought.

"I'm looking for a motive. If she did, then perhaps there's another family member out there who wants the inheritance too. It might explain the attack. Has anything like this happened before?"

"No." Naina mulled over the possibilities. "Besides, my grandmother didn't have much financially. Just a small house and a few personal things. We weren't wealthy by any means."

Abhay ran a hand through his thick hair. He actually wanted to move his hands through her hair. "Do you know anyone who would want to hurt you? Any enemies? Co-workers or clients you've made angry in the past?"

I know where you live. Devender Singh's threat echoed in her ears. Still, she hated to accuse him of trying to hurt her when she had no proof.

"Naina, if you want me to help you, you have to trust me," he said covering her hand with his.

"All right," she began, "In my business, I've made a few clients angry, inspector."

"If we're going to be working together, I'd rather you call me by my first name," said Abhay, beginning his flirting speech.

Naina couldn't resist a smile.

"I'd like you to send me a list of all your clients, and highlight any client or their partner who haven't been pleased with their settlement," Abhay said. *Aur main unki maar lunga*, he thought.

"And what about boyfriends? Any lovers or exs we should worry about?" Abhay wanted this information more for personal reasons than official ones.

Naina tensed. How in the world was she supposed to answer that? "No," she said softly.

There wasn't a man in her life! A ridiculous sense of relief filled Abhay. He felt like standing up on the table and start dancing like Shammi Kapoor. '*Yahoooo, chahey koi mujhe jangli kahey.*'

Naina thought she saw the inspector smile and she couldn't help it herself.

Abhay was losing himself again. "Do you know that you look beautiful when you smile..."

Her lack of a boyfriend eliminated the possibility of an ex-lover trying to hurt her, but he had a disturbing feeling that wasn't the reason he was relieved. She made him feel really alive. Actually she made junior feel really alive. He realized. *Damn.* He couldn't do this. He could get sucked in by her. She was just a case. A strange, bizarre, and fascinating case.

As they stepped out of the café, his gut told him that something was wrong. He had to listen to his instincts. Why was something nagging away? Why was that little bell at the back of his head ringing insistently, warning him something was wrong?

Two goons came out of nowhere and blocked the way. Abhay saw two men standing thirty steps away in the dark, silhouetted against the glow coming from the street light. The guy on the right was in his mid-thirties, judging by his posture, medium height, thick upper body, a bizarre shape to his head, because of uncooperative hair. He had the kind of hair that should have been cut much shorter or atleast shampooed everyday. The inspector's face went tight, but after a couple of seconds he relaxed and forced a smile. He could understand that these goons had come to hurt Naina, but obviously he wouldn't let them do so.

The guy on the left was tall, but nonetheless a fat, grunting figure. "*Abey Inspector! Ladki humarey hawaley kar dey.*"

A malicious smile slithered across Abhay's face as he walked up to them. "*Tum kya ladki key mama ho, jo ladki tumhein dedoon?*" He took off his scarf and tied it on his wrist.

He looked at Naina who looked bewildered and scared. He threw the car keys at her and she caught them. "Here! Switch on the music in the Jeep and enjoy," Abhay said.

Naina rushed to the Jeep and put the keys in and turned. The music started playing automatically, at *shadi*-volume. She wondered what this craziness was about, but stayed glued to the seat.

> *"Feel the heat, feel the kick, feel the power,*
> *feel the punch! Aao ji, bauji, dil se dil milao ji,*
> *aa gaya hai dekho bodyguard."*

Abhay smiled and half-turned, and like he knew they would, the two guys moved towards him, ready to grab him. Abhay leaped up in the air and planted a long left hook at the left hand guy. *Dhishum.*

It caught him hard on the ear, and the guy's head snapped sideways and bounced off his partner's shoulder, by which time Abhay was already throwing a right-hand uppercut under the partner's chin. *Dhishum.* The guy's head went up and back the same way his buddy's had bounced around, and almost in the same second. Like they were puppets, and the puppeteer had sneezed.

Both of them stayed on their feet. One of the men was wobbling around like a man on an unsteady boat, and the right-hand guy was stumbling backward. The left-hand guy was all unstable and up on his heels and his belly seemed inviting.

Abhay popped two solid punches into his belly, hard enough to drive the breath out of him, soft enough not to kill him. The guy folded up, crouched and hugged his knees.

And the car stereo continued booming.

"Sab se hot, sab se hard Jo bura hai uski waat
Aa gaya hai dekho bodyguard."

Abhay stepped past him and went after the right-hand guy, who saw him coming and swung his right hand to hit him. Abhay dodged him and lifted the man from his neck, banging him on the floor. *Wham!*

Abhay heard Naina's scream and he saw a masked man standing next to her. He ran towards Naina. The masked man ran away on his bike. Abhay realized it was a getaway plan, but it was too late. He spun around towards the other goons and saw them disappearing into a black mercedes which had appeared out of nowhere.

"The *chaiwala* hasn't come today, so we won't get any chai, Shukla. You'll have to make it manually, which I trust is not beneath the dignity of a constable. Make tea enough for four." Mishra grinned and lowered his head, returning to his typewriter. He was the Head Constable and knew where to use his powers.

Shukla was at his desk, trying to dig himself into the files in order to look busy, but failed miserably. On hearing Mishra's comment, he looked pathetically at him.

Mishra raised his head. "You needn't get your beard wet with tears over such a small thing, my little hairy son. Is there a problem, constable? Something in your orders that you don't understand?"

Shukla's face was rigid with fury. "You want me to make the tea?" He said it as if he had been asked to strip.

Mishra returned Shukla's glare with a scorcher of his own. "Yes, constable. Any objections?"

"Yes," snapped Shukla, jerking a thumb at a young constable, who was hovering by the lobby door, with his *danda,* anxiously peering out into the road. "What about him? Why can't he do it?"

"Because he is doing a very important job of keeping the police station safe, with his *danda*. And anyway, why should he be the tea boy instead of you? You're both the same rank ... you're both constables or have you forgotten?"

As if the bugger would let him forget! He spun on his heels and barged out of there, slamming the door behind him.

Mishra heard darogaji's Jeep approaching, and adjusted his uniform, and made his back straight. The phone on his desk gave a little cough. Mishra glowered at it, daring it to ring. It defied him. So did the other phone. Damn and blast! He'd planned a quick exchange of dialogue with Inspector Abhay in which the inspector would look around the empty station and say, "All on your own, Mishraji?" and he would reply smartly, with much diffidence, "Yes, sir, but I can cope. I can run this place single-handed if need be." And the Inspector would smile approvingly and make a mental note that there was some very promising promotion material here. Instead, Inspector Abhay breezed through, nodded curtly at Mishra and said, "Those phones need answering, Mishraji."

Mishra picked up the phone. The man on the phone sounded out of breath and was barely whispering into the phone. "*Sirji, meri bhains ki chori ke baarey mein kuch pata chala?* Could you find my buffalo or the thief?"

Abhay smacked the files on the table. "Can I get some *chai*?"

"Shouldn't be long, sirji," said Mishra, adding with a note of smug triumph, "Shukla's making it."

Abhay stepped back in amazement. "How did you get him to do that?"

"Simple. I gave him an order. Why shouldn't he make it? He's only a bloody constable."

"He may be a bloody constable," said Abhay, "but half the time he thinks he is an inspector."

Mishra smiled and called out loud, "Shuklaji! How much longer are you going to be making that bloody tea?"

Abhay lowered his eyes guiltily as Shukla handed him the mug of tea; he kind of had a soft corner for Shukla. "*Itni badhiya chai banai hai,* Shuklaji. Looks good."

Mishra, looking up from his typewriter, said, "Thanks very much, Inspector... sorry, I mean constable," which provoked a muffled snort of suppressed laughter from everyone.

Shukla's face went tight. *Laugh, you bastards. My time will come. Dekh loonga ek ek ko.* Shukla made a note.

Even though Shukla got on his nerves sometimes, Abhay knew his worth. Shukla was old in the system and had the knack of getting information on people quicker than anyone else in the force. He also understood Shukla's scepticism about Naina, and Shukla had a right to his doubts. Shoot, even he had doubts.

"Okay, Shuklaji, what have you found out?" Abhay said sipping his hot tea.

Shukla pointed to a file on his desk and started in his familiar drawl. "The post mortem report of the body in the public toilet has come in. As per the report, the death was because of an accident with a car. I checked but no one has reported seeing an accident in the last one week."

"Hmm. And what about Naina?" Abhay asked.

Shukla started again in his monotonous tone like an erstwhile newsreader. "Got some background on Naina, sirji. She left a big corporate office with a booming practice to start her own firm here in this small town. Doesn't make sense why she would do such a thing. Okay, divorce cases are rising here too, but they are definitely not as high as Mumbai."

"Any problems with co-workers there?"

"No, sirji. Her boss said that she was a brilliant lawyer, but also mentioned that she kept to herself. Thought she was a little weird, but didn't say anything specific."

Abhay found a half-smoked cigarette hiding in his pocket and lit it gratefully. "Did he know why she decided to leave the practice?"

"No. Her boss seemed shocked, said her announcement came out of the blue. He even offered her a raise, but she refused. Sirji I am telling you, *woh ekdum pagal hai.* Believe me."

Abhay drummed his fingers on the file. Why had she left such a good position to move back here? To the town where her parents were killed, to a house that must hold haunting memories for her? Was she running from someone or something back in Mumbai?

"Oh, and her colleagues said that her move had something to do with her boyfriend, too. Apparently they had a big fight before she left. His name is Ashish Luthra."

Abhay swallowed a cloud of smoke as he squashed out his cigarette in a saucer. *Bahot achhey! Humsey hoshiyari.* How could he have been so stupid to believe her! He was furious with himself for being so gullible. If she'd lied about having a boyfriend, what else was she lying about? *Bahot tez cheez hai yeh ladki. If she can play this game, then even I can.*

Naina was mesmerized by the lavishness of Uncle Chauhan's mansion. She had never seen anything like it. She had read a feature about this home in some magazine, but it didn't do the real thing any justice. With its imported marble and fixtures, elaborate decorative mouldings, and its extensive gardens dotted with statues and fountains, the house was like a five star hotel. She made her way up the driveway and rang the doorbell. A servant answered it and led her to a lounge where she waited for Uncle Chauhan.

The split-level lounge, which ran almost the full length of the ground floor, was roomy enough to park an aircraft. It smelled strongly of expensive leather, rich cigar smoke, and money... lots of money.

Naina waved to Uncle Chauhan and he crossed the carpeted floor of his elegant lounge and approached her; a brilliant smile spread across his face. Dressed in all whites – kurta, pyjama, and juttis – he truly looked distinguished and evermore the politician.

"It's good to see you, my dear," he said, giving her a kiss on her forehead. "Come, let me introduce you to everyone." He extended his arm to escort her into the enormous main dining room where a crowd of similarly dressed guests were chatting or nibbling away at the array of snacks situated artfully on white linen-covered tables or being served on silver trays by waiters dressed in black. A massive crystal chandelier sparkled above the room giving the place the feel of glitz.

An uneasy feeling flitted over Naina as she joined the party. Tension crackled through the air. Hushed murmurs and curious stares met her appearance.

"Relax, my dear, they won't bite," he whispered in her ear.

Naina laughed. She had always liked her uncle's sense of humour. Naina tried to relax, but she felt like an unwelcome outsider. When he introduced her to his guests, she sensed tension in their tight smiles and nods. They knew who she was, knew about her past. Some of the people had probably known her parents. Coming back home had been a huge mistake. Could she really deal with all the gossip and curious stares directed her way?

When the small talk had died, Naina found herself staring vacantly at the party. Uncle Chauhan chatted away with a friend beside her.

A familiar face wedged its way into the sea of people. The lounge doors crashed back on their hinges, and in came Inspector Abhay Pandey. With him was the bearded Constable Shukla. He was looking like an overgrown, sniggering schoolboy who had been invited to the birthday party of a rich friend.

Abhay was wearing a black leather jacket, white shirt, with a pair of jeans. The jacket brought out the contours of his broad shoulders and the light made his bronze skin glow. This man was sexy beyond any man she had ever encountered.

Slinging the scarf round his neck, Abhay yelled for a waiter to get him some whiskey.

She looked around the room and a strange feeling swept through her. It was as if someone was watching her. She knew this feeling. It started the week she had moved back home. She'd considered reporting her fears, but she had no proof. And she knew the police wouldn't believe her. Naina shook the thought away and tried to bring herself back to reality.

"Do you know that man?" Naina held Uncle Chauhan's elbow gently and whispered into his ear.

"Of course! Wherever there are politicians, there will be police officers. That's the way it goes. Also, you're forgetting that I know almost everyone in town," he said with a chuckle.

"I think your profession has ruined you. You haven't had the time or inclination to get married?" he continued.

Naina took a glass of juice from a passing waiter. She was surprised at the sudden question. "No. I'm not sure marriage is for me."

"Why do you say that, my dear?" Uncle Chauhan asked, concern dotting his eyes.

"I'm independent, I have my own business, friends. I don't need to be married," she said although she wasn't very convinced herself.

While they were busy chatting, an elderly woman with gleaming white hair, dressed elegantly in a black sari with diamond rings in her fingers, just passed them by. Uncle Chauhan stopped her.

"Mother, this is Naina Sinha. You remember her?" Chauhan swept a hand toward Naina. "Naina, this is my mother, Suchitra Devi Chauhan," Uncle Chauhan quickly added.

The old woman's pale coloring turned a pasty white. "Yes, I remember something about her," the woman said in a low voice, peering at her. "Nice to see you, Naina. Amazing how much you look like your mother." Suchitra Devi said in a clipped tone and hurried away, making Naina wonder if she'd somehow caused the woman to be uncomfortable.

Uncle Chauhan tried to control the situation. "Have you made any friends here? Anybody I might know?"

Ria didn't count and nor did Inspector Abhay Pandey. "Well, not yet. I've been here only a short while."

"Well, I'd like to be this girl's friend," a drunk voice boomed beside her.

Naina jumped at the sound of the deep voice. Another *bewda*, she thought.

"Girish!" Uncle Chauhan turned as a tall, dark-haired man slapped him on the back.

"The party's great, Dad," Girish said as he raised his glass in the air. "But who is this beautiful woman?" Girish's wide grin showed off a set of perfectly straight and polished teeth. A politician's smile like none other.

"This is Naina Sinha," Pradeep Chauhan said, giving him a stern look.

Girish's ignored his father's look. "It is a pleasure, Ms Sinha. Welcome to our home."

"Excuse us for a minute," Uncle Chauhan said, deftly guiding Girish away so that he wouldn't cause him more embarrassment.

"I'll definitely see you later, Naina," Girish said, flashing her a smile as he was being led away.

"I didn't realize you knew ex-MP Pradeep Chauhan," a familiar voice said to her.

Naina turned to find Inspector Abhay looking at her.

"He's like my godfather. He was a friend of my parents."

"I see," Abhay said as he had a swig of his drink. "I can see you need more than one man to satisfy you. First Ashish, and now Girish. *Hmm badhiya hai.* Ever thought of trying both of them at the same time?" He said with a sly smile on his face.

"What a barbaric thing to say!" Naina was taken aback for a moment when she saw the grinning inspector. "I didn't mention about Ashish, because I know he is harmless and...."

She was cut off mid-sentence, as just then, a woman called out to Abhay.

Abhay continued smiling. "We'll finish this discussion later. Actually even I can't be satisfied with just one woman. We have a lot in common."

He watched the woman approach them. Her soft scent, her lips, her blue sari hugging her curves, her blouse cut deep to show off her ample cleavage – confidence radiated from her every pore. With jet black straight hair bouncing on her shoulders and a figure to die for, she was gorgeous. Her eyes sparkled with pleasure when she saw the inspector.

Though Abhay wasn't too keen on getting too friendly with her, he took the opportunity to play his side of the game with Naina.

Naina caught sight of Abhay staring at the woman in wide-eyed approval, his tongue almost hanging down to his stomach.

Tara Chauhan took Abhay in her arms and hugged him, patting his butt and murmuring words that meant nothing to Abhay but sent razors towards Naina.

"Do you know Tara Chauhan?" Abhay asked her.

Naina shook her head. She knew that Tara was Uncle Chauhan's daughter, but they'd never met before.

"She's gorgeous," Naina said, wondering if the inspector had dated her.

"Definitely, she is the most beautiful woman I have ever seen," said Abhay, rewinding his scarf. He turned to Naina like a stage artist awaiting an ovation

Hearing this compliment, Tara gave Abhay a kiss on his cheek and then manoeuvred her way between Naina and Abhay. The smooth silk of her dress slid against his hands, "Hi, Abhay. Good to see you again," she cooed.

"*Khushi toh mujhey ho rahi hai tumsey milkar,*" Abhay said. Her hazel eyes, more green than brown, watched him. Her soft black hair cascaded around her face, the fiery waves tempting his hands to smooth them back from her flushed cheeks. He pursed his lips when he saw her breasts moving quickly beneath her dress, her nipples poking impatiently at the light fabric.

Naina tensed and watched Tara give Abhay an appreciative look but she composed herself and extended a hand. "Hi Tara. I'm Naina Sinha. Your father and I..."

"I know who you are," Tara said in a sweet but abrupt way.

"My father told us you were coming. It's nice to finally see you. Perhaps we can go out for coffee together sometime," Tara suggested.

"Sure. That would be lovely," Naina said, a little confused if Tara meant what she said. She had met a lot of rich people in Mumbai and was aware of the small talk they made at parties.

"Why don't we have a drink..." Tara purred into Abhay's ear.

"I'll ask the waiter to get you one?" Abhay suggested.

Tara's ruby red lips formed a perfect pout. "Okay."

At the far end of the hall, Shukla was busy stuffing himself with snacks of all sorts. He was gulping down expensive scotch, like there was no tomorrow.

A man walked up onto the platform and silenced the crowd to begin his speech. He looked like a member of some political party. He started speaking and Naina realized that the speech was all about Girish and the wonderful future that lay ahead of him.

Naina found the opportunity she had been waiting for to make her escape. She quickly slipped out of the crowd and headed to the door. As she approached the exit, she was surprised to see her office assistant in a corner with Girish. They seemed to be in deep conversation. She hadn't realized that Ria knew him. She started towards them to go and say hello, but changed her mind and decided she really was ready to leave.

While Abhay was busy flirting with Tara, Naina had reached home.

Just as she finished changing her clothes, the telephone rang. Naina looked at her watch and reached out for the receiver.

"Hello, we are speaking from Blossoms Flower Delivery and we need to deliver some flowers for you. Our runner would be reaching you in some time. Hope that's fine with you ma'am?" A young boy's voice said.

"Yes, I am home, but who has sent the flowers?"

Even before she finished her sentence, the young boy had kept the phone down.

Naina got worried after the gift in the office episode, and called up Abhay, asking him to come over.

Abhay was enjoying his drinks and was in no mood to leave the party for the drama queen Naina. But somewhere deep down, he also wanted to go to her, and he did.

She came out wearing jeans and a white T-shirt that were perfectly moulded over her rounded breasts. She'd scrubbed her face free of makeup and had removed her shoes. Abhay didn't know why he found her being barefoot so sexy, but he did. He shifted on his feet, reminding himself of the reason for his visit.

"What happened? Why did you call me at this hour? I have other things to do than just solve this case," scoffed Abhay.

Naina walked across the room, putting some distance between them. "I don't want you to get wrong ideas. I need your support and would like to give you some more details. It could help you crack the case."

Ab aaya oonth pahaar ke neechey, Abhay thought.

Applauding loudly, Abhay walked from the doorway to the couch. Then he turned around and made a circle with his forefinger and thumb. "Perfect, darling, absolutely perfect. Now we are talking." Abhay sat down on the couch and lit up his twentieth cigarette of the day.

Naina started her side of the story. "Well, as you already know, Ashish is my ex-boyfriend. We dated for a while and then he started getting obsessed with me, so I left him. But believe me, I don't think he is dangerous."

"Aashiq hai Ashish. Hmm." A long silence stretched between them. Abhay wasn't so sure. He'd been a cop too long. A rejected lover or boyfriend could mean trouble.

Naina hugged her arms around her in a protective gesture. "I think someone's trying to drive me crazy."

Abhay narrowed his eyes. *"Decide karlo.* Is someone trying to kill you or are they trying to drive you crazy? Which one is it, Naina?" Abhay puffed out smoke rings almost as large as car tires.

Naina shook her head. They were interrupted by the sound of the doorbell. Naina went to get it. She requested Abhay to come with her.

"Who is it?" she asked, her hand on the doorknob.

"Florist delivery service," a young male voice answered.

Abhay opened the window and hurled out his cigarette, then leaned forward and peered along the drive. When he saw the truck with the Blossoms logo on it under the streetlight, he nodded for her to open the door.

The young man was wearing a green cap with the word 'Blossoms' printed on the front. He held up a long white box with a pink ribbon tied around it. "Your lucky day, er, night," he said, grinning.

"Thank you," Naina said as she took the box from him.

Abhay pinched a few notes out of the *chhamiya* fund and handed it as a tip to the boy. The delivery boy was surprised with such a big tip, much more than the cost of the flowers. "Thank you *sahab*. God bless you."

Abhay had his own ways of helping people.

She carried the box to the dining table and lifted the lid. Tears pooled in the corners of her huge eyes. "Oh my God," Naina whispered. "Who would do such a thing?"

The box was filled with crushed sunflowers.

"But what does this mean…" Abhay was puzzled by the supposed threat.

"Sunflowers are my favourite flowers. I used to always carry a bunch with me as a child. My grandmother told me that…" Naina cradled her head in her hands as she spoke, her voice desolate. "Why is this happening to me? Why?"

Abhay heard the frustration, the fear, the agony in her voice. He couldn't stand it. The smart thing to do was not to get involved. But then again, he didn't always do the smart thing. He mostly just listened to his gut instinct. And right now, his gut instinct was screaming at him to comfort her. He took her in his arms and held her.

"I don't know what's going on, but we'll get to the bottom of it," Abhay said in a quiet voice. He gently traced his thumb along her chin and tilted her face to gaze into her eyes.

Being held in Abhay's arms was definitely not calming. This was dangerous territory. Desire laced his husky voice. His lips were a mere whisper away, his breath hot on her skin. Naina's breasts pressed against the hard wall of his chest. Heat skittered up her spine, and the rough texture of his stubble on her cheek sent a hot need through her.

"Tell me not to do this," he whispered as his lips grazed her hair.

"Abhay, I—" Naina's unspoken argument died when his warm mouth met hers, sending a rush of pleasure and passion through her. His mouth devoured hers, his lips daring and forceful as he claimed the tender recesses of her mouth with his plunging tongue. Naina's body reacted to his need by moulding to his hard masculinity, and a low moan escaped her when his lips moved to the delicate skin beneath her jaw.

Abhay's hands lingered at her waist as he touched his forehead to hers and exhaled loudly. His words came out on a ragged breath. Instead of releasing her, Abhay continued to stroke her back as he had before, slowly allowing the tension to ease from both their heated bodies. When he finally looked at her, she saw a mixture of the passion they'd ignited along with a strong sense of regret, but he still didn't let her go.

"I'm sorry. I shouldn't have done that," Naina said. "Because you are working on my case; not because it wasn't good."

Abhay wondered what she was saying. *Kya bol rahi hai! Case gaya bhaad mein.* He definitely didn't want to stop.

Beneath her thin t-shirt, her nipples stood erect against the soft cotton, and her breasts ached for Abhay's touch, a realization that shocked her. But she gave Abhay a hard, assessing look, then dropped her hands to his side. "I think we should stop."

Abhay wanted to push her on the couch and go his way. But he also stopped. He knew this heat which had been generated would come out soon and it would be more enjoyable when both parties would be ready.

He covered her small hand with his own. "Trust me, Naina," he said and left.

If only she could trust him.

The next morning, Abhay slipped into his police uniform, his favourite red scarf and holstering his gun, he headed to his jeep.

At the police station, he began his investigation of Ashish. It wasn't because the guy had been involved with Naina personally, but because it was the logical place to start the investigation. He had asked Shukla to prepare a file on the guy. Abhay studied the data. He kept going through the papers till something caught his eye. Ashish was one of Mumbai's leading architects and had great knowledge and information about his company's land investments. A small subsidiary of the company had accused Ashish of embezzling funds. *Mr Ashish toh khiladi bhaiya hain,* he thought.

The case had gotten some local media attention, but had ceased just as suddenly. He skimmed through the next few editions of the paper and discovered a small section explaining that the company had reached a settlement and the charges had been dropped.

Abhay ran a hand through his hair and leaned back in his chair, placing his booted feet on his desk while he considered the possibilities in the *tik tik tik* noise of the typewriter.

Did Naina know about Ashish's past? Perhaps Naina had accidently discovered something about his business and Ashish might be worried about her disclosing the information. If his career was at stake, he had a viable motive. It was a theory worth investigating.

Shukla came in grinning.

"You look happy, Shuklaji," commented Abhay. "Your beard's gone all stiff.

Shukla checked his beards with his hands. "Sirji, I have some great news for you which will close this Naina case. *Aur bhi toh case solve karne hain, sirji. Aakhir ek aadmi ki bhains chori ho gayi hai.*"

Abhay laughed at his comment. "*Kya baat kartey ho Shuklaji.* I was in such a serious mood and you just changed everything. Tell me what news you have."

Shukla continued moving his fingers in his beard. "Sirji, I visited the Blossoms florist shop as per your instructions. The owner told me that the sunflowers were already wilting and he was about to throw them out but the customer insisted on buying them. Paid for them in cash too."

"And who was the customer?" Abhay asked impatiently.

Shukla tapped his forehead in thought. "Umm... sirji, that guy told me that it was a girl. She had long black hair and dark eyes. And yes, she was wearing a brown jacket with a peculiar brooch on it. The shopkeeper remembered that it was in the shape of some bird, like a peacock."

"How does this news solve the case, Shuklaji?"snapped Abhay.

"Sirji, I am telling you Naina is insane, and is doing all these things herself."

Naina woke up and looked outside her window. Every day in Allahabad had been an eventful one. She wondered what was in store for her today.

She dressed carefully – brushed her hair, put on some makeup – but no matter what she did, when she looked in the mirror, all she saw was a ghost. Naina got to office, poured herself some tea and waved to Ria who was busy on the phone. Before sitting down, she took off her jacket to hang on the chair and noticed that it was already occupied by her brown jacket. She was surprised to see her brown jacket there. She didn't remember leaving it at work. She threw her jacket across the table and started her work. She was engrossed in her papers when the phone rang.

"Naina, it's Uncle Chauhan. I wanted to make sure you got home all right."

Naina's fingers tightened around the handset as the memories of the crushed flowers came back to her. "Yes, I'm all right, why wouldn't I be?"

Uncle Chauhan hesitated. "Well, I couldn't help but notice that you seemed a little tense at the party. Now that you're in town, I intend to make sure you're taken care of."

Naina fiddled with her pen and smiled. "I'm fine, uncle. It's really sweet of you to ask."

"Listen, I'd like to have dinner later in the week. How about Friday?"

"Sure," Naina said and hung up. She turned back to her file but felt someone's presence in the room. Abhay was standing in the doorway. He was looking devastatingly handsome today, Naina thought. "Hi," she said, fumbling with her pen and dropped it. Naina couldn't read his expression, but the smile she'd seen last night when he'd asked her to trust him was absent from his eyes.

Abhay paused by her chair. An odd expression crossed Abhay's face. "Whose brooch is that?" he asked, his voice clinical, as he pointed to her brooch.

Naina swallowed. Abhay's cold, formal tone surprised her. Where was the man who'd been so sensitive last night? The man who'd kissed her and awakened her needs. She reminded herself that she had no reason to be afraid of Abhay. He was here to help her. "It's mine."

Abhay's unreadable expression turned into a puzzled frown. His long fingers stroked the colourful peacock brooch on the jacket.

Naina got up to explain. "This brooch belonged to my grandmother. She used to be mad about the vibrant colours of peacock." She looked at the brooch and then at Abhay. "What's wrong, Abhay?"

When he spoke, his voice was harsh. "Constable Shukla checked with the florist. He said the person who ordered those flowers was a woman in a brown jacket with a peacock brooch just like this one!"

"You think I sent the flowers to myself?" Naina finally asked in a dull voice.

Abhay wound his scarf tighter and buried his hands deeply into his pocket. He chewed his bottom lip and said nothing. The disappointment in her eyes almost softened his resolve, but he now knew better. Even if it meant discovering she was a liar.

"You're just like everybody else. Once you've heard about my past, you decided I was crazy." Naina's dark eyes blazed with fury. "Yesterday you asked me to trust you, and today you accuse me of sending myself a box of dead flowers."

"I'm not accusing you of anything. I intend to find out who's behind all these things, Ms Sinha."

"Good, because I want them to stop."

"So do I."

"Good."

"Fine."

A strained moment stretched between them. Finally, Abhay lowered his voice and said, "I checked in on your boyfriend–"

"Ex-boyfriend," Naina clarified.

"Okay. Did you know he had been charged for embezzlement?"

"Those were dropped. Besides, that happened in Mumbai. I don't see how that can possibly be related to what's going on here," Naina said tightly.

"Did you and Ashish ever discuss business?"

Naina's tone was sarcastic. "Not confidential matters if that's what you're implying."

"Bear with me for a minute, Naina," Abhay said, reining in his temper. "If Ashish was involved in something illegal, and...if you inadvertently were privy to some information, Ashish would have a motive to come after you."

Naina mulled over the possibility. "I suppose it's possible, but I don't remember anything. The only thing Ashish told me about was a few investments, but I don't remember the details. Anything else?" she felt frustrated by his questions.

Abhay gritted his teeth. Yes, he wanted to kiss her and taste the fire in her body. But that was impossible. He didn't even know if she was telling him the truth.

"Look, Naina–" A knock at the door made him stop. A good thing, he thought, before he made a fool out of himself.

Ria stuck her head in. "A gentleman's here to see you, Ms Sinha."

"Send him in," she said.

Naina was surprised to see Girish Chauhan.

Gentleman? Ghantaa! Abhay thought.

Girish flashed Naina a leering smile. And she returned it with a warm one of her own.

"What I see I like," said Girish his eyes moving from her to the bookshelf.

"Thanks," Naina said, unsure whether his compliment was for her or the furniture.

"Mr Abhay Pandey, I have heard that you are taking too much interest in Naina's case," Girish said sarcastically.

"*Meri toh yeh duty hai,* but what are you doing here? Don't you have an election to win?" Abhay looked at him and smiled.

Girish stood face to face with Abhay and said "Abhayji, if inspectors like you spend most of their time behind a girl's skirt, criminals *ka kya hoga?*

"*Desh ke neta bhi usee skirt mein ghusenge to desh ka kya hoga,* you think about that," said Abhay, tucking his scarf inside his collar as he walked out of Naina's office.

Naina quickly asked, "How come you are here?"

Girish leaned against the wall, trying to act casual. "I was in the area and dropped by. I wanted to take you out for lunch."

Naina folded her hands across the top of her desk. "I really have a lot of work to do."

Girish grinned and sauntered toward her. "Well, you have to eat too and it might as well be with me."

Naina smiled. "Shouldn't you be someplace doing social work and impressing people?"

Girish's rich laughter filled the room. "I don't think it'll hurt my image to be seen with a beautiful woman."

"I see," Naina smiled in spite of his remark. "So you wanted to talk business?"

"No, I want to relax and enjoy myself, and get to know you better. After all, you're special for my dad. That makes you someone special for me too."

The thought of refusing Girish's invitation struck Naina as a good idea as she could smell alcohol on him. But she'd promised herself she would associate with the people from her past. Perhaps Girish had heard his dad talk about her parents, and she could learn something that would trigger a memory. She agreed and picked up her bag.

Downstairs, a sleek black Mercedes gleamed in the afternoon sun.

"Very impressive," she said as she sank into the plush leather seats.

"Father bought it for me as a present." He pressed a button and a tray opened with a bottle of champagne and two glasses. He poured it into two glasses and offered one to Naina.

The driver quickly manoeuvred the car onto the road, and a few minutes later and two glasses down, they were settled at a table in at the restaurant of the Royal Cliff. This was the best amongst the two five star hotels in Allahabad.

"This is great," Naina said, admiring the ambience of the restaurant. "I've heard about this place, but I've never been here before. "Turning to Girish, she initiated conversation," Why don't you start by telling me about yourself?"

Girish had already ordered a scotch for himself which he gulped down in one shot. "My life's an open book. I'm sure you've read all about it in the papers," he said through a grin.

"Yes, but tell me about growing up. Are you and Uncle Chauhan close?"

Girish's smile faded slightly. "As close as a father and son can be. There's always that parent-child thing."

Naina studied his face, wishing she understood the parent-child thing.

"I'm sorry," Girish looked contrite. "That was insensitive of me. Father said you don't remember your childhood."

A wave of apprehension rippled through Naina. "That's right. At least not the first five-six years."

Girish pushed his stylish glasses up on his nose. "Is that why you came back here? Hoping to remember?"

Naina picked at her food. "That's part of it. I hoped moving here would bring back memories, but so far it hasn't."

Girish gulped down another glass of scotch.

Bewda! How could a politician openly drink in the afternoon? Naina wondered. She looked around and saw that the restaurant was empty. This was probably his den for his afternoon drinking sessions.

"You know, I've been thinking," Naina said, "I know a lot of my father's stuff was confiscated by the police. I think some of it may be with your dad too as he was a great friend."

Girish arched an eyebrow. "I don't think my father has anything. Do you think it's a good idea for you to pursue all this? I mean, what possible reason would you have to look into your father's old stuff?"

Naina sipped her water and decided she'd said enough. "Anyway, maybe I'll talk to Uncle Chauhan about it."

A muscle tightened in Girish's jaw. "I doubt father would remember anything. He's getting up there in age now, you know. And he is really busy with the campaign."

Girish's barrage of excuses made Naina uncomfortable. She studied his easy smile, and she was sure that he was putting her off. She checked her watch. "I need to get back to the office. I have an appointment at three."

Girish paid the bill, and Naina stiffened when he placed his hand on her back and guided her to the car. *Kamina.*

When he dropped her at her office, he tried to kiss her, but Naina quickly stepped away. He frowned and as he walked back to his car, he said, "Maybe next time."

Ya right! On your death bed, loser, Naina thought as she watched him drive away.

Abhay drove down the winding road to State Bank of Allahabad to meet Devender Singh. Although Naina had insisted she had no enemies, after studying her client list, he'd noted a couple of possibilities. Devender Singh topped the list. Abhay parked his jeep right outside the bank, music blaring in his stereo:

"Yahan bhi hoga wahan bhi hoga,
ab to saare jahaan mein hoga Kya...
mera hi jalwa...jalwa...jalwa..jalwa."

He was surprised to see that there was no security guard at the gate of the bank. That seemed out of place. Just when he had taken a step or two towards the gate, the guard in a shabby uniform and *danda* in his hand came running from the nearby *paan* shop and greeted daroga babu with a salute.

He ignored the guard and dashed into the bank; he was here for something else. *Guard ki class kisi aur din,* he thought. The staff told him that Chief Manager Devender Singh had been on leave for a few days. So Abhay entered Devender's room and examined the man's desk, skimmed the papers on top, searched through his files, then rummaged through the top drawer. While he was searching the files on his desk, a piece of paper slipped to the floor – it was a familiar news clipping about Naina's past. Her home address was scribbled in red ink across the top.

Within seconds, he'd ordered a search on Devender Singh. Maybe he'd been wrong to suspect Naina. Both her prior boyfriend and Singh had possible motives to harm her.

Abhay summoned courage to knock the door of his police service quarter. He knocked and waited.

He could hear footsteps and then he heard the door unlock. The door opened and his mother stood in front of him. An old lady, with grey hair, sincere eyes, wearing a cotton sari. Before Abhay could say anything, she welcomed him with a light slap on his left cheek.

"*Time milgaya ghar aaney ka? Hotel bana ke rakha hai ghar ko.*" She chided. "Why didn't you come home yesterday? I was waiting for you."

"*Woh Maa kya hua ki...*"

She cut him off saying, "Don't start any of your stories and come inside."

Abhay came and sat on one of the chairs along the table.

"I have made your favourite Paneer Pasanda *aur namkeen paranthey*. Quickly wash your hands and come." His mother said, as she entered the kitchen.

Abhay smiled. "*Kya baat karti ho maa tum bhi, gussa bhi aur pyaar bhi.*"

Ria had left for the day and Naina was packing her stuff to leave for home.

"Naina?"

She recognized Abhay's deep husky voice immediately. It sounded so different from Ashish's wimpy voice, and it was much sexier and more masculine than Girish's fake polished speech. She closed her eyes, trying to tamp her emotions.

He came in and walked towards her. "I went to see Devender Singh today."

"You did?"

"Yes. Apparently he's skipped town." Abhay pulled the scrap of newspaper from his pocket. "And I found this on his desk."

Naina took the paper and saw her name and home address. She saw the article about her and gasped. "He knew about my past!"

"That's right. About your parents...and your amnesia."

"Do you think he's the one who's been taunting me?"

Abhay shrugged. "It's possible."

The telephone rang, interrupting the strained silence.

"Naina Sinha speaking." She heard deep breathing, then a fuzzy, unrecognizable voice.

Abhay must have read the distress on her face, because he punched the speakerphone button immediately.

"Leave the past alone," the voice said.

"Who is this?" Naina asked. Her hands began to tremble.

"Someone who knows all about you. Someone who wants you out of Allahabad." The phone clicked into silence.

Abhay had to believe her now; he'd heard the man's voice himself. "We'll find out who the caller was," Abhay said, pressing the button to show the caller's number.

As the phone number blinked before her, Naina covered her mouth and gasped.

"What happened? Do you recognize this number?"

Her voice came out in a choked whisper. "It's...it's my residence number!"

She raised her fear-stricken face to his. "Someone made the call from my house!"

Abhay put his hands around her arms. "Even if we rush now, the person would have left. We are dealing with a very smart mastermind here. *Bahot chalak hai sala.*"

Naina nodded. Her face was pale as a sheet. "I don't understand why this is happening."

"Someone is certainly using your past to hurt you," Abhay said, thinking of the range of possibilities that existed.

"My past has always controlled my life. I have to face it and bury it so I can go on," Naina said exasperated.

"What are you talking about?" Abhay asked.

"You know, I can understand why I blanked out that night," Naina said in frustration. "But why the rest of my childhood? I don't even remember living here."

"Maybe there's a reason you can't remember. Do you want to talk about it?" he asked.

She looked into his eyes, its dark rich colour drawing her in with its tenderness. "I had these nightmares as a child," she finally said. "I still have them sometimes."

"What happens in them? *Batao mujhe.*"

"I see a shadow suffocating me to death. I try to escape from the clutches of the shadow but it suffocates me, tearing the life from my lungs as someone thrusts a bloody knife into me. I open my mouth to scream, but the sound gets caught in my throat. My parents... They are going to die and there's nothing I can do to save them. I want to run for help, but something blocks the doorway. I crouch into a ball and hide in the darkness, biting my lip until I taste my own blood, covering my ears to drown out the pain of my parents' cries. I couldn't save them. The sharp sound of someone's shoes scraping along the floor makes my flesh crawl. A loud thump follows. I'm in the bedroom with my parents lying on the floor...but there's someone else there. I can see a shadow."

Abhay traced his fingers along Naina's hand, opened her palm and twined her fingers with his. "Then what happens?"

"I don't know," Naina says, her hands clenched in frustration. "I can't see the person's face. I try and try but I can't and the doctor said it was just a figment of my imagination."

"The police didn't find evidence of anyone else being there that night?"

"My grandmother said they didn't. That's when they ruled it out. But I know there was someone. I mean I think–" She broke off, unable to finish the sentence.

"I know," Abhay whispered. He rubbed her shoulders and wiped the tears from her eyes.

"Do you believe me?"

Abhay chewed his lip. "I want to help you find the truth. Isn't that what you want?"

Naina nodded and lowered her eyes. He hadn't exactly said he believed her.

"Let me drop you home so you can get some rest," he suggested, fighting the urge to take her into his arms.

When they were home, Abhay continued his questions. "I know you're shaken, Naina, but I have one last question. Does anyone else have the keys to your house?"

"Yes, but that's just Ria. She needs to get papers and things if I am ever out for a meeting, you know."

Abhay dialled Shukla's number and briefly told him about the threatening call. "Shukla, I need some fingerprint assistance. Get here quickly with the expert. Also you need to do a background check on Ria Sood, Naina's assistant. I want to know everything about her." He then turned to Naina and said a bit reluctantly, "I'd like to talk to Ria."

"Sure…" Naina dialled Ria's phone and told her about the phone call.

Abhay heard Ria's shriek. *Drama queen huh!*

"I'm fine," Naina said. "But Inspector Abhay Pandey wants to talk to you." Naina handed him the handset.

"Ria, have you given your set of keys to Naina's house to anyone? Or lost them?"

"No, I haven't!" Ria was baffled by these questions.

"Kya baat kar rahi ho! It's so strange," Abhay said. "Naina's house has been broken into twice, and on both times there were no signs of a forced entry. It's almost as if the intruder had a key and you say that you have no idea. *Ek lady constable bhejoon tumhare paas kya?"*

"No, no, Inspector. I don't know anything about that," Ria said, sounding slightly defensive.

Could Ria be involved? Abhay wondered. *What motive would she possibly have? Kaatil type lagti toh nahin hai.* The doorbell rang and Naina went to get it. Shukla and a young, uniformed officer were at the door. He saw the wide frown Shukla gave Naina and noticed her posture go rigid in defence.

"I want you to check for fingerprints around the house," Abhay said to the expert.

The fingerprint expert put on his gloves and began combing the place.

Later, after Shukla and the expert had left, Naina went to her bedroom and said to Abhay, "I think I'll take a bath and try to sleep.

"Do you want me to stay?"

Naina's head snapped up. As she stared at him with a multitude of questions in her eyes, he instantly realized what she thought he'd implied.

"I meant…until you get through." He shifted from one foot to the other, not looking at her. "I thought you might feel safer that way. *Main toh bas vaise hee keh rah tha,*" he grinned.

A tiny smile played on her rosy lips. "Thanks. I do feel safe when you're around." Then she turned and hurried into the bathroom.

Abhay sat down on the couch. He heard the water running, and he could picture Naina stripping down to her beautiful nothingness and slipping under the shower, her rosy nipples taut and glistening with water, her bare wet legs begging for his touch. Junior was getting edgy in his trousers. He muttered a curse, then settled onto the couch and covered junior with a cushion. Naina felt safe with him. But she wasn't really safe with him. He wanted to take her to bed and show her his raging desire. He bit his lip and waited for the water to turn off, silently praying that she had not locked the door.

Naina relaxed under the hot water and stared at the unlocked door, wondering if Abhay had seen the flicker of need she'd unveiled before she'd rushed into the bathroom. She was too afraid to ask him to join her, too afraid he would say no. Her body tingled with anticipation at the mere thought of him sitting on her sofa while she stood naked under the shower. What would she do if he opened the door and joined her? Naina grabbed her robe, embarrassed at her sinful thoughts. If he wanted her, he would make a move, and obviously he hadn't. She slipped on her silky robe and combed the tangles from her wet hair.

Junior was not going to get suppressed by a cushion. As junior moved to his senior position, Abhay rushed inside the room and turned the bathroom door knob. He wanted her with an intensity that made him question his own sanity. The bathroom door opened and Naina stepped out from the bathroom, her hair wrapped turban-style in a towel, her creamy skin glowing.

Uff little late ho gaya. Chalo koi baat nahi, he thought. He swallowed a groan and closed the distance between them. He traced one finger down her jaw, then lowered his mouth to hers. Gently, he savoured the yearning he felt in her response, the soft moan that escaped as she parted her lips and teased his mouth with her tongue. She tasted sweet, and his ache for her grew as he deepened the kiss. She caressed his jaw with her soft palm, and he thought he would die from the raw need that surged through him. He pulled her tight against him, wrapping his arms around her waist. Naina clasped her hands behind his neck and swayed with him to the seductive rhythm. Nuzzling his throat, she inhaled his masculine scent. Smooth skin greeted her questing lips as they strayed across his jawline.

Abhay and Naina lost themselves in each other, allowing their hands and mouths to explore each other with tantalizing slowness. Naina slipped her fingers inside his shirt, caressing his broad chest and six pack abs. His low hum of approval encouraged her, and she slid her hand lower. He stroked her breast through the soft material of the gown. Naina gasped and arched her back, pressing forward. Gorgeous. The woman was absolutely gorgeous, and he'd never get enough of her. Abhay reached around and removed the towel from her hair.

"Look at me, Naina."

Her eyes met his, sparkling like jewels.

Shoving the thin strap of the robe aside, he planted smouldering kisses along the slope of her shoulder and she shuddered in response. He removed the other strap, and the robe slipped from her body to pool around her ankles. Abhay let his own clothes fall to the floor. For a moment, everything stopped as he admired her naked form in the moonlight. A heartbeat later, he scooped her into his arms and placed her in the middle of the bed. She reached for the sheets.

"No." He stopped her hands. "I want to see you all of you." He set off in a slow exploration of her body, touching every inch of her and revelling in the experience. The lavender perfume she'd chosen suited her perfectly and drove him wild. He was determined that this night would wipe clear any memories she had of other lovers. He might not be her first, but by god, he'd be the one she remembered for the rest of her life.

Her moans and tiny whimpers of response pleased him. Her hands skimmed his shoulders as he kissed a path down her flat, smooth stomach. She twitched beneath him and gasped, then went deadly still. He smiled in anticipation. He caressed her in the most intimate way, slowly.

She bucked, clutching the sheets and gasping his name. It sounded even sexier when she couldn't catch her breath. He continued his loving torment until her entire body tensed in climax, and then she collapsed, panting for air.

"That...that was..." she said weakly.

"Fabulous?" he offered, grinning up at her.

A satisfied smile lit her face. "Definitely fabulous."

"Do you think you can get some sleep now?"

"I think so," Naina smiled.

"I'll be here all night and open for round two. But I will be gone early in the morning."

Naina toyed with the bed sheet. "Thanks for staying."

He nodded, studying her. She looked more relaxed and calm. Abhay gathered her once more into his arms. In no time, she was fast asleep.

As Abhay studied the files Shukla had left on his desk, he rubbed his hand along the new crisp red scarf around his neck. He could smell Shukla's smoky breath before he heard him speak.

"Constable Shukla reporting, sirji."

"Got anything on the results from that knife we found in Naina's house?"

"Only one blood type identified. Ms Sinha's." Shukla spoke like a military officer.

"No other blood type? Did you get the results of the DNA test?"

"DNA tests indicate the possibility of another person's blood on the knife, but the tests are inconclusive. Also, I've got that report on the fingerprints, sirji. Only fingerprints in the house were hers, yours and someone else's," Shukla said. "We couldn't match the last one. Whoever touched them isn't in the system. Also sirji, someone from forensic department should be here soon. They'll be able to tell us in more detail, you see."

"Yes, they're such clever bastards," commented Abhay, who had little time for the geniuses of the forensic section. Abhay fiddled for his cigarettes.

"Any news on the accident report of that man we found in the public convenience?" Abhay asked.

"Yes, sirji. Last week we received an anonymous call that a black Mercedes had hit a man on the same street. But no identification has been given. I got the call traced but it was from a phone booth near the same *Sulabh Shauchalaya*."

Abhay gave his forehead a wallop with his palm. Then he saw Shukla's shoes – scuffed, unpolished, and water-stained from the public convenience adventures. If there had been time, he would have insisted that Shukla polish them and give his uniform a thorough sanitation. But there wasn't time.

Abhay puffed his cigarette, contemplating his next move. Naina had been certain she'd cut the intruder's arm. *Back to square one,* he thought. "I need you to run another check for me. Pull up anything you can find on Naina Sinha. I need to know everything about her life after she moved to Mumbai with her grandmother. Also, Devender Singh has disappeared. Find out where he is."

"Sirji, I will get to the bottom of it." Shukla spat his tobacco aiming right outside the main gate in the flower pot. His aim was very good. At least with the tobacco spit.

"Good morning, Ria," Naina said as she stepped into her office. "Uncle Chauhan, what are you doing here?" She was surprised to find him there.

Her uncle's warm smile wasn't as bright as usual. He got up and gave her a hug. "I came to visit you. Anything wrong with that?"

Naina shook her head. "No, of course not."

He shoved his hands in his pockets. He looked tired and worried, and Naina suddenly felt sorry for him. "Is there something wrong, uncle?" she asked as she settled at her desk and motioned towards the visitor chair.

Uncle Chauhan shook his head and sat down. "I've actually come here to talk to you about Girish."

"Okay," Naina said, unsure where he was going with this.

Uncle Chauhan gave her a shaky smile. "I know Girish took you to lunch the other day."

"Yes."

"I'm not sure that you and he...well, that you should–" he coughed, struggling for words.

"That we should what, uncle?"

"That you two should get involved."

"Involved? What do you mean?" She stood up, hands on her hips, and glared at him.

"Girish's in the middle of an important campaign, and there's enough gossip already about his drinking habits. I don't want any more gossip happening."

Naina was stumped by this. She thought her uncle was the only person in town she could trust. She thought he loved her. But she realized that when it came to his family, she was an outsider, someone with a past that could hurt his precious son. "Don't worry, Uncle," she said in a hard voice. "I don't plan to get romantically involved with Girish."

"Wait, Naina," he sounded desperate. "You don't understand.'"

"Oh, I understand perfectly," she said, walking towards the door and opening it for him. "I really have to get back to work now, Uncle."

Uncle Chauhan frowned, his grey eyebrows knitting together. "I'm sorry if I've offended you, my dear. That wasn't my intention."

"It's fine," Naina said, forcing a smile.

Uncle Chauhan stopped for a moment. He looked like he wanted to say something else, but shook his head and walked out the door.

After finishing her work, Naina called Abhay over. She didn't want to be alone and after her talk with Uncle Chauhan, she felt rattled. Abhay junior was more than happy to accept the invitation.

"Thanks for coming," Naina said softly, raising her dark eyes to look into his.

They were sitting in the living room and Abhay's eyes were drawn to the old cartons once again. He couldn't help but ask her. "What do you have in those cartons?" Abhay said, pointing to the unopened cartons tucked away in the corner of the living room.

"I've never opened them but I know these boxes have my grandmother's stuff."

"There might be something in there, *dekho toh sahi,*" Abhay said.

Naina had come to Allahabad to deal with her past. The odd circumstances surrounding her had frightened her, but she was tired of being scared and alone. It was time for her to take control of her life. Abhay seemed like a man she could trust, at least with her past. But with her future, she wasn't sure. She would have to be careful not to fall for him, to guard her heart as she always had. He was a man who played with danger every day, a man who was too experienced for her, a man who would move on when her case was over.

Naina lifted the sheets of newspaper covering the contents and looked inside. The first box had a family picture on top. She pulled it out and examined the faces. Her mother had been a beautiful woman. Naina had her dark hair, slender build, porcelain skin and the same black eyes. Her father was handsome too, with black hair, a moustache and grey eyes that held a commanding look in them. His nose was prominent and his jaw wide. He'd been a tall man, overshadowing her mother's small frame. In the picture, Naina was wearing a frilly red dress and was sitting on her father's lap with sunflowers in her hand. She loved sunflowers. It amazed her that she could see the whole family together, but she had no recollection of posing for the picture.

"You're beautiful, just like your mother," Abhay said, his voice rich with playfulness.

Naina nodded solemnly. She'd almost forgotten he was there.

Abhay gave her an encouraging look and she pulled out a scrapbook. It had dozens of pictures of her and her parents. Some were of her as a baby, then a toddler at a birthday party they'd planned for her. A few pages had blank, faded spots as if photos had been removed. Naina wondered who had taken the pictures out and why.

As she studied the photographs, something struck her. "That's odd."

"What?"

"My parents were so close to Uncle Chauhan, I wonder why there aren't any pictures of him in here."

"Hmm. He was a Member of Parliament back then, wasn't he? He probably was busy in his political affairs.

Naina closed the book. "Maybe you're right."

Abhay picked up a diary. "What's this?"

"Looks like my father's appointment diary."

Abhay studied her father's diary and made a note of all the appointments Mr Sinha had the weeks prior to his death. Interestingly enough, Suchitra Devi Chauhan, Uncle Chauhan's mother, had scheduled a meeting with him only two days before he had died. *Had the woman been soliciting campaign contributions for her son or did she have some other business in mind?*

He also made a note of the fact that Mr Sinha was one of the few attorneys in town twenty years back, so most of the people probably consulted him on legal matters. It was likely half the town had made appointments with him that month.

While Abhay was lost in his thoughts, Naina extracted a sealed envelope and opened it. It contained her parent's marriage certificate and her birth certificate. She'd been born on first May at Allahabad Community Hospital, weighed four kilos and had been twenty inches long. She traced her finger along her parents' marriage certificate, pausing when she noticed the date of their marriage. Her parents hadn't been married until first October, just seven months before her birth. That meant her mother was already pregnant when they got married! Swallowing her surprise, she quickly stuffed the certificate back in the envelope before Abhay could see it. She had enough of her past to be ashamed about. She didn't want him to know that on top of everything else, she'd been conceived even before her parents got married.

He motioned to the envelope. "What's in there?"

"It's just my birth certificate," she said softly. "Well, I guess that's it," Naina said, getting up from the floor.

Just then, the phone came to life. Naina picked it up to hear a man's agitated voice. "Naina, this is Ashish. I don't know why you haven't returned any of my calls, but I want to talk to you. It's been two months now."

She sighed and ran a hand through her hair. "I'm sorry, Ashish, I haven't called, but my schedule's been crazy and I had to get settled and..." She rattled out excuse after excuse, while Abhay lifted up a banana from the fruit basket on the table and started enjoying it. He wondered what Ashish was saying on the other end of the line.

"No, please don't come here," she said. "Listen, Ashish, I really can't talk now." A long pause followed. Naina lowered her voice. "Yes, it's business. Can I call you back?" She said and hung up.

Business, huh? Abhay thought. Junior definitely wanted to do some more business with her.

"So, is Ashish coming here?" he asked, hiding the banana skin behind the flower vase.

Naina shook her head. "I don't think so."

Abhay nodded, wondering if Naina would be interested in some more 'business' right now.

The station lobby looked as tired as Abhay. The flowers which had been placed on his order in the lobby were making it look more like a dreary tomb. Only two men were on duty, Head Constable Mishra behind his typewriter and Constable Shukla.

Abhay dropped his cigarette end to the ground and crushed it under his heel as he lumbered into the police station. Head Constable Mishra, sad-faced and balding, raised his head to the ceiling and then back to his typewriter.

Shukla unaware of the inspector's arrival was busy fiddling with his beard.

"Don't just sit there plaiting your beard, Shuklaji. Do something useful for a change," Abhay snapped.

"Couldn't agree with you more, sirji," replied Shukla, ignorant of what Abhay had said.

"So what's the update on the case?" asked Abhay.

"Sirji, with great difficulty we have been able to solve the case completely." Shukla spoke in an excited tone.

"What, how...!" Abhay was baffled.

"Sirji we have retrieved the lost buffalo! The case file is on your table. The owner was very happy and has given us four litres of milk as a gift." Mishra spoke in one go.

"What milk...what buffalo?" snorted Abhay. "I am asking you about the Naina Sinha case, any update on that?"

"Oh that! Yes sir, yes sir. You had asked me to check about Ashish." Was Shukla's unhelpful reply.

"And what did you find?" Abhay took off his scarf and placed it on the table.

"Ashish! Sirji, he is pretty boring. I could fall asleep just talking about him."

Seeing Inspector Pandey smile, he continued, "Ashish goes to work at eight, has lunch in the office cafeteria every day, he works late, goes to a local gym once or twice a week, orders dinner in every day from some local restaurant. And that's his life in a nutshell. *Ek number ka fuddu aadmi hai woh sirji,*" Shukla said pulling a fake yawn.

"Any women in his life?"

Shukla chuckled. "No Sirji! I told you he's *fuddu*. Nothing interesting in his life."

"And he's been in Mumbai all week?"

"Until three days ago. After that he has left for some business in Fatehpur."

Hmm. Fatehpur was just two hours away from Allahabad for Ashish to drive down, thought Abhay. He had also contacted Naina. What if he had been right here in Allahabad? It now seemed like a possibility.

"Ek baat toh bataana bhul hee gya. Lucknow police have found Devender Singh," Shukla said, leaning against his desk, "in some motel. Holed up with a *chhamiya.*"

Abhay blushed remembering his hot night with Rani. "How the hell did they trace him there?" Abhay asked.

"His wife. She is a very nosy woman. She had a private investigator on him the whole time as she was going through the divorce and wanted some solid evidence to get freedom from that ass."

"Hmm, very good job Shuklaji! So he's been there since the day he has been missing?"

Shukla nodded. "That's correct, which means he's probably not responsible for the incidents happening with Naina."

"Maybe, maybe not. He could have orchestrated the whole thing from the hotel."

Naina glanced at her watch. She had a little over half-an-hour before she'd have to meet Tara Chauhan, Uncle Chauhan's daughter, for lunch. She still hadn't understood the woman's phone call this morning and her insistence on the meeting. She seriously couldn't understand what she wanted to discuss.

After wading through her morning paperwork, a slight headache started to nag her. She was ready for a nap, not lunch with Tara Chauhan. She didn't know what she was possibly going to talk to her about all through lunch.

"I'm taking the afternoon off," Ria said, poking her head into Naina's office. "I made some fresh tea if you want some."

"Thanks, Ria. You are ever so kind," said Naina, grateful for Ria's thoughtfulness. She filled another cup and sipped, the hot brew calming her.

"And Tara Chauhan called and said she'll see you at that Coco Brown Café around the corner," Ria said and left.

Meeting Tara was intimidating and she wanted to look her best. Naina finished her tea, ran a brush through her hair, retouched her makeup and headed out to meet Tara. When she got to the café, she found her waiting at a corner table.

Tara beamed as Naina walked over to greet her. She was wearing a stunning green silk sari. Her diamond bracelets jangled as she shook Naina's hand.

"Hi. Great café," Naina said.

"I love this place," Tara said, settling down in her seat again. "The coffee is fabulous and some of their dishes are just divine." She nodded toward an already-filled mug. "I took the liberty to order us coffee."

Naina had just finished her tea in office but she didn't want to offend Tara, so she smiled and sipped the coffee. After they ordered the food, Tara unfolded her napkin and toyed with the long diamond studded loop dangling from her ear. "I thought we should get to know each other."

"Really?" Naina couldn't hide her surprise.

"Yes. Daddy's talked about you for years, and Girish mentioned he took you to lunch the other day."

Oh boy, here it comes, Naina thought.

Instead, Tara flashed her a sugary smile. "I remember Daddy telling me about this one time when you were little... Your parents brought you to one of his parties and you followed me around all day."

"I did?"

"Yes, isn't that cute!"

"I...I suppose so." Naina did a quick mental count. When she was six, Tara would have been eighteen. She could see how she must have been drawn to her.

"Anyway, I'd forgotten all about that," Tara said.

Naina laughed softly. "I must have been a pest."

"Not really. So, after the campaign party the other night, Daddy told me what a tough time you had after your parents died, when you went to live with your grandmother," Tara said sympathetically.

Naina couldn't help but feel she was being sincere. She swallowed several sips of coffee, hoping to dislodge the lump forming in her throat.

Tara gave her a sympathetic look. "What made you decide to move back after all these years?"

Naina had expected subtlety. But this woman had no qualms about asking what she wanted to know. "I wanted to work for myself instead of a large firm," Naina said, sipping her coffee.

"Yes, but you could have done that anywhere. Why come back to this town? You must have bad memories." Tara brought her hand to her cheek in a dramatic gesture. "I just can't imagine it."

"That's just it," Naina said, meeting Tara's curious gaze head-on. "I don't have any memories of this town at all."

"None?" Tara asked sympathetically.

"None at all," Naina said matter-of-factly.

"So when those doctors said you suffered from amnesia, it was true. I thought they were just making it up."

"It's true," Naina said, suddenly losing her appetite. "I've tried everything to remember but nothing has worked." Naina's head was starting to throb even more, and she began to feel nauseous.

"But I see you've already found a man. You're seeing that handsome inspector, aren't you?" Tara said with a wink.

Naina took a sip of water. "He's a...Tara, I'm not feeling well at all...' Naina said, massaging her temple as a wave of pain rocked through her. "I am feeling a bit dizzy."

"Oh, dear! What happened? Do you want a medicine for headache?" she said quickly rummaging through her bag.

"No, no that's okay. I have something at home. I think I just need to lie down."

"I'm so sorry. Do you want me to drive you back?" Tara seemed concerned, and Naina felt even worse for skipping out on their lunch. Perhaps she and Tara could be friends, after all.

"Actually I had a headache when I was in office. It's just become worse now," Naina said getting up. Her head was becoming blurry. She wondered how she was going to drive back home in this state.

Tara walked Naina to her car. "I hope you feel better. Let's do this again sometime soon."

"Sure," Naina said.

She blinked to ward off the dizziness. With great difficulty, she drove her car back to office, breathing deeply and trying to suppress the throbbing at her temple. She clutched the stair railing and slowly climbed the steps, then shuffled into her office by sheer willpower. Two painkillers later, she stretched out on the sofa and fell asleep.

Naina awoke with a start to the sound of a tree limb scraping against the windowpane. She looked out of the window at the darkening sky. Her heart was pounding, her breathing erratic. She covered her face with her hands and took several deep breaths to remind herself that the dream was over. It was just a dream – just like she'd had thousands of times before. She looked at the clock and groaned. 8.30 p.m.

She padded into the bathroom and washed her face, then retrieved her keys and purse and a few files to work on at home. Switching off the lights, she made her way down the stairs. The remnants of fatigue and her earlier headache weighed on her body, and her muscles felt heavy.

She shivered and glanced around for other people, but the parking lot was amazingly empty so early on a Friday. It looked like it was going to rain. Hurrying home would be best. She got into the car, fighting with the wind as it caught a few strands of her hair and swiped them from her topknot. Something white caught her eye. A towel lay in the passenger seat, all wrapped up.

She hadn't put it there. Reaching across the seat, she slowly unfolded the edges of the towel, her heart thumping as a red stain came into view. The ends of the towel flopped open and she saw the shiny glint of metal. Blood trickled onto the soft leather of her car seat, and a scream got locked in her throat. It was one of her kitchen knives, covered in blood. Just then, someone grabbed her arm and Naina screamed.

"Naina, what the hell is wrong?"

She turned to see Ashish standing beside her car. She wondered where he had landed from, but pointed with unsteady hands towards the seat.

Ashish couldn't understand what Naina was trying to say. But he spotted the bloody knife and understood that something was wrong. He helped her out of the car. "Come on, sit in here." He gently led her into the front of his own car and then reported the incident to the police station.

"How are you in Allahabad?" Naina said, scared. She remembered Abhay's theory that Ashish could be behind all this.

"I will explain all that later," said Ashish as he pulled Naina into his embrace, and she relaxed against him, grateful for the warmth of his arms. His arms were not as strong and warm as Abhay's and she wished Abhay was here to comfort her. She really needed his embrace.

"I want to know why you're here." Naina asked Ashish as they entered her home.

Ashish sighed and pushed his black-rimmed glasses up on his thin pointy nose. "I was worried about you. I couldn't figure out why you wouldn't return any of my calls."

"I told you when I left that it was over between us, Ashish. That I wanted to move on."

"I know," Ashish said. "But I thought once you got here, you'd miss me and change your mind. But I guess you haven't been lonely and have found someone else."

"It's...it's not what you think."

"Come on, Naina. I'm not stupid."

She ran her hands up and down her thighs in a nervous gesture. "Well, maybe partly. But there's more." She went on to explain about the attack and the threats she'd been getting.

Ashish's already-fair skin turned ghostly pale. His eyes bulged beneath his glasses. "Oh my God! You think someone's trying to kill you?" he said finally.

Naina shrugged. "Or drive me crazy. I really don't know what to think, except I think everything may be related to my past – the parts I can't remember."

She started to explain, but Ashish stopped her. "I know about your parents, Naina. You already told me and I understand your pain."

92

"How long have you been in Allahabad?" Naina asked.

"A couple of days," Ashish said, looking sheepish.

"So you were here in Allahabad when you called me?" Naina asked.

Ashish nodded. "Yeah, I was missing you and wanted to ask you if I could come over, but you sounded too distracted. I couldn't figure out what was going on."

"I'm sorry, Ashish," Naina said quietly. "I really am. You're a good friend, but like I told you in Mumbai, that's all it can ever be.

Ashish finally stood, threw up his arms in a gesture of defeat and opened the door.

He leaned over and kissed Naina on her cheek. "I hope you find what you came here for."

Shukla stood in front of Abhay's desk while he was busy working on some case files. Shukla was whistling happily as if someone had tipped him a fiver.

"I figured out something today, sirji."

"What?" Abhay asked as he puffed his cigarette.

"Naina is right-handed. I have seen all her pictures and she is holding things in her right hand."

Abhay's eyebrows shot up. "Oh? And how is that so important to our case, Sherlock?" Abhay played along, though he already knew what he was trying to say.

"When her wrist was cut during that first attack, it was her right hand wrist. If a right-handed person tried to commit suicide, she'd cut her left wrist, not her right. It's only logic, sirji."

"That's brilliant, Shuklaji! You are so sharp." Abhay said in a mocking tone as he took a long puff of his cigarette.

Shukla made a sullen face. *Why did he always end up in the inspector's jokes. As if his beard jokes weren't enough!*

"Stop being dramatic, Shukla!" Abhay snapped. "Did you find anything from the prints off Naina's car."

"Her office assistant's prints were one of them. You asked me to check into her, too."

"Ria's prints were on Naina's car?" Abhay wondered.

"Yes, sirji, but she works with Naina, doesn't she? Maybe she took something to her car for her."

"It's quite possible she did."

Shukla licked off a trickling bit of tobacco liquid from his lips. "Also, she has been seen with Girish many times and that too very late at night. Do you think she's a possible suspect?"

"Interesting, but it's her motive that I can't seem to understand." Ria Sood worked for Naina, had access to her keys, her car and perhaps her house. But why would she hurt Naina? After all Naina had given her a job.

"We've also got back the final report on the bloody knife in the car," Shukla said. "Blood was from a butcher shop, not a human's."

"So, someone is trying to drive Naina crazy. Hmm."

"Sirji...I also found this I-card of Ashish Luthra in the car." Shukla informed in an uninteresting tone.

Abhay snorted out a lungful of smoke and jumped up from his seat. "What! Ashish Luthra! Naina's ex-boyfriend? You had said that he was a *fuddu* guy with no life at all. And look, his I-card is found in the same car as the bloodied knife. We can never stop doubting until we find the culprit, Shuklaji. Please find this Ashish guy and interrogate him."

"Funny you should say that, sirji. Even I was thinking same to same." Shukla grinned and continued. "I will action it immediately, haven't done third degree since many days." Shukla smiled and looked at his bamboo *danda*.

"No third degree! Just check with Naina about Ashish's whereabouts and then question him." Abhay said assertively, "And I am going to check out Suchitra Devi and Girish Chauhan, as they had met Naina's father just before his death as per his diary. The key lies in discovering who is threatening Naina. Once we figure that out, we'll know who was responsible for murdering her parents."

Naina was leaving her office when the phone rang. She hurried back to answer it. "Naina Sinha speaking."

A cold and clipped voice replied, "Ms Sinha, this is Suchitra Devi Chauhan, Pradeep Chauhan's mother. My granddaughter Tara told me she had lunch with you yesterday."

"Well, it wasn't exactly lunch. I'm afraid I wasn't feeling too well and had to leave before our food arrived."

"Here's the thing: I'd appreciate if you would stay away from my family. With Girish running for the Member of Parliament, our family doesn't need any negative publicity right now. You understand, don't you?"

"What?" First Uncle Chauhan didn't want her to see Girish, now his mother wanted her to stay away from the whole family.

"Murdering your parents was bad enough, but I won't let you harm any of my children."

Naina gasped. She'd heard rumours of people calling her a murderer, but no one had ever said it to her face before. Anger quickly replaced hurt. "I understand your concern, Mrs Chauhan, but I don't have any intention of interfering with your family. Thank you for calling." Naina said politely and slammed the phone down on the old cow.

The music blared from the jeep stereo

"Apna kaam chalta, bhaad mein jaaye janta
Ye desh tha veer jawaano ka Ab reh gaya
beimano ka…"

Abhay smiled at the aptness of the song as he drove towards the Chauhans' residence. Somehow he had never liked politicians.

He wanted to pee so he parked his jeep and decided to commune privately with nature behind a convenient bush in their house, too modest to flaunt his equipment. An odd little smile twinkled through his face as he zipped up and walked across the lawns to the main gate.

The Chauhan family was one of the richest families in Allahabad, and Suchitra Devi knew everyone who was important in town. She was a society matriarch and would do anything to ensure her alcoholic grandson's future in politics. *To what lengths would she go to protect her family,* Abhay thought, as he reached the door. A servant greeted him at the door and showed him to the formal sitting room where Suchitra Devi Chauhan was. She was wearing a designer golden sari and heavy gold jewellery, and even at her age, she looked royal and quite formidable. The diamond studded rings in every finger, her shrewd eyes and pointed chin added to the aura.

It was time to dive in without knowing how deep the water was. *Jo hoga dekha jayega!* Abhay thought.

"I think your family is making a lot of money in politics." Abhay pointed towards her diamond rings. *"Kuch paisa gareebon key liye bhi chhor diya karo."*

"What we do for the poor is talked of all over. Don't you read the papers?"

"Newspaper toh neta ki jageer hotey hain, jo marzi likhwalo," Abhay retorted as he moved his hand on his scarf.

"Inspector!" Suchitra Devi shouted as she stood up from her chair. "For a public servant, you're bloody insolent."

"Itna gussa sehat ke liye acha nahin hai devi ji. Just chill chill... just chill!" Abhay hummed as he poked a cigarette into his mouth and scratched a match on the table.

Suchitra Devi's eyes spat fire. "I find you offensive."

"Then you're in good company, Suchitra Devi. Mind you, I find it offensive that rich people can kill innocent people and get away with it." Abhay lined up the ends of his scarf.

"Let's come to the point." Abhay fiddled with his cigarette. Smoke drifted from Abhay's mouth and lazily twisted and turned.

"What can I do for you, inspector?"

"I want to discuss something that happened a few years ago."

"Is this about Naina?"

"Kamaal hai, aap toh antaryaami hain." Abhay grinned.

"I saw the two of you flirting at Girish's party."

"*Badhiya hai!* When you know so much, then please throw some light on her parents' murder case also."

The woman's lower lip curled into a look of disdain that only a true snob could pull off. "It was a horrid thing that happened; I feel sorry for that poor child."

"I believe you and your son visited her in the hospital shortly after the incident."

Shock widened the woman's eyes momentarily, but she quickly masked it and fanned her face, her diamonds glittering as she waved her hand back and forth. "Yes, my son was...worried. And in his position, we thought it was a good to show concern for the child," she said.

"So, you did it for making the news?" A bitter taste filled Abhay's mouth. "*Kaminey neta log,*" he muttered, adding a salvo of smoke rings to the already murky atmosphere.

The old woman smiled, glad he understood.

"Mrs Chauhan, Mr Sinha's diary indicates that you and your grandson visited him the week before he died."

A blush tinged the old woman's white pallor as she dug her bony fingers into her lap. "Yes. He was one of the few lawyers in town. He handled some legal affairs for us."

"And Girish? He was only...what, around twenty back then?"

"Nineteen, but he was already part of a youth party. Mr Sinha was overseeing its legal executions."

The quickness of her reply struck him as odd, almost as if she'd practiced her response. Also, she seemed to have an answer for everything. *Chalak hai budhiya,* he thought.

"Inspector Abhay Pandey, I hate to bring this up after what happened to the poor family, but I was withdrawing my accounts from Mr Sinha. There were rumours that he was sharing confidential information to the opposition party. But when we stopped business with him, it might be possible that someone from the opposition party killed him as he didn't provide the information even after taking money from them. And my family certainly couldn't have had our name associated with someone like that," the old woman said.

Abhay studied the old woman. She was cunning and definitely out to protect her family. But at what cost? "And you think that might be the reason for his death?"

"Who knows?" The woman toyed with the diamond rings on her hand. "Or perhaps someone found out and Mr Sinha was so distraught, he killed himself. Politics can be a vicious game...Or he was involved with the wrong people and they murdered him."

What a witch! Or rather a bitch. Abhay wanted to send Suchitra Devi to Shukla's third degree cell. He thought that was the only place where this bitch would speak up. He imagined Shukla beating her up with his bamboo *danda.*

"Was your son Pradeep Chauhan here the night the Sinhas died?"

"Oh, no. He was away on the campaign," she said examining her nails. "But he came back right away to check on the child."

Abhay got up. He'd had enough of her and her crap. "Is your son here?"

"No, he and Tara are hosting a charity event tonight."

"*Kuch kaam bhi kar liya karo, bas charity function karte rehtey ho.* What about your grandson Girish?"

Even though she was acting to be as cool as a cucumber, anxiety streaked Suchitra Devi Chauhan's face for an instant. "He's in his office, but I believe he's busy at the moment. You could make an appointment with his secretary."

"Appointment toh mainey iss duniya mein aaney ka bhi nahi liya, bas aa gya." He snapped as he walked towards Girish's office.

Outside Girish's office, he saw Girish's secretary – a sexual fantasy of nineteen or twenty. She stopped him from entering inside. "You can't go in without an appointment."

He observed the sexy secretary who was trying to stop him. His appraising glance covered everything from the top of her head to her tiny waist. It took in the expensive dress which she wore, and the gold necklace and earrings which seemed like expensive gifts given to her for some favours she would have bestowed on Girish.

Sensing she was being observed, she tore her eyes away and heaved herself up out of the chair. Her eyes flickering curiously, she asked, "Girish sir is busy for this week. Should I book an appointment for next week?"

All he was checking out were her nicely shaped breasts. He wondered how they would fit in his palms. Abhay looked at her breasts and then at junior, and then finally at her face.

"I need to see Girish Chauhan," he said as he moved towards the cabin door.

"We do not accept walk-ins, under any circumstances, inspector."

"That's good," Abhay replied with a little heat. "But I am not asking you, just telling you baby." He winked to her and walked past her and kicked open the door. *"Mera jab man chahey, mein tab wahan ja sakta hoon.* It's better if you remember – I go where I feel like, when I feel like." Abhay walked inside majestically, and made sure his statement was heard by Girish as it was intended more for him than for his sexy secretary.

"Oh, it's you inspector. I didn't see you. What brings you here?" Girish asked flashing an uncomfortable smile.

Abhay made himself comfortable in one of the leather chairs and put his feet up on the table. He briefly explained to Girish about his investigation into the Sinha case. "I wondered what business you had with Mr Sinha years ago." There was the rasp of a match as Abhay lit his fifteenth cigarette of the day. Girish edged the ashtray forward to receive the spent match, but was too late. Abhay's foot ground the carpet, and the smell of burning wool joined the other aromas.

Girish's smile slipped slightly. "I didn't have business with him," Girish said. "I was just a young boy then."

Abhay hesitated, remembering Suchitra Devi Chauhan's story. "You didn't go to see him about handling your youth party's legal affairs?"

Girish looked puzzled for a moment. "Oh, yes, I did. Although I don't remember what day it was that I was scheduled to see Mr Sinha. If I remember correctly, I don't think I ever made it to the meeting."

"Are you sure you didn't meet him at all that week? *Soch lo, nahin toh merey paas aur tareekey bhi hain sach ugalwaaney ke.*" Abhay gritted his teeth.

Girish ki fatt gyi. He stammered. "No, no. Not at all. Now, if there isn't anything else, I have an important meeting to go to."

Abhay grinned. He knew Girish was lying but he thought it was enough for the day. He stood up to leave. "*Phir milenge,* very very soon."

Abhay dialled Shukla's number as he sat in his jeep. Could Suchitra Devi Chauhan or Girish possibly be responsible for everything that happened to Naina – her parents' deaths, the threats, the attack, the tape recorder, the crushed flowers? But if they had killed her parents and didn't want her to remember, why send her things that might trigger that memory? Unless...unless they thought she was unstable and might become so distraught that she'd take her own life. He certainly didn't like that line of thinking.

Abhay reduced the volume of the jeep stereo as Shukla received the call. *"Kya baat kartey ho Shuklaji.* Why were you not picking the phone? Have you left the police force or what?" Abhay said, as he steered his jeep out of Chauhans' mansion.

"Sorry sirji, *woh baat nahin hain na.* Actually Mishraji had ordered me to make some fresh tea with ginger. He has a bad throat, you see. So both my hands were occupied," Shukla replied hastily.

"Did you do some work, or just kept making tea?"

"Sirji, *kaam hum poora karte hain, by God ki kasam.* I had brought Ashish in for interrogation, but even before I used my *danda*, he started crying like a wimping kid. Even Mishraji could have taken Ashish down with one simple blow and the man would never know what hit him." Shukla said in a single breath.

Abhay grinned at Shukla's comment. "How did his I-card reach Naina's car?"

Shukla continued, "Sirji, he said he had dropped it when he took Naina home that day. I have even checked his fingerprints and they don't match with those on the knife. Even Naina called to say that Ashish is incapable of killing anyone."

Abhay thought, *So he took her home. Hmm. Lagta hai pyar abhi baki hai.*

The car stereo hummed at low volume:

"Oh womaniya, aah aah womaniya,
badley boyfriend badley apna saiyaan.
oh womaiya aah aaah womaniya."

The jeep bumped on a speed-breaker, breaking Abhay's chain of thoughts. "Did you find any information about Ria Sood?"

"Sirji, she's not at her place; her house has been cleaned out."

What in the hell did Ria Sood have to do with all this? Was she a paid assistant in someone's demented game or was she some psycho who had planned the whole scheme to torment Naina on her own? But why would she do something like that? Abhay wondered.

"Also, I found out that when she'd come to Allahabad, she volunteered on Girish Chauhan's campaign, and learned some general office skills along with some bedroom skills while working with him. You know what Girish's motto is."

"What motto?" Abhay asked.

Shukla continued in a sing- song manner: *"Apun ko toh chahiye, din mein special chai; shaam ko daaru, raat ko ladki, aur neend aa jaye.* Sirji, all he needs is alcohol and girls. From there, Ria had taken the job with Naina. So her connection to the Chauhan family is Girish, not Suchitra Devi. I think when Naina returned, Ria helped

Girish torture Naina because she was physically involved with him. A logical reason for a girl like Ria."

Naina looked out of the window at the fading sunlight as it formed shadows on the lawn. *Just like in her nightmares,* she thought. In every shadow she thought she saw the silhouette of a man. She was more certain every day that the vision in her dreams was the man who'd killed her parents. And if she could just remember that night and see his face, she could make him pay for destroying her life and murdering her family.

The phone rang interrupting Naina's thoughts.

"Naina, it's Uncle Chauhan."

"Hello Uncle," she said cautiously. She wasn't sure what to expect after his last phone call.

"Tara told me that she enjoyed having lunch with you."

"Yes," Naina croaked.

"I'm so glad that you both are friends. I'm calling to invite you and a date, of course, to my house for a private dinner party tomorrow night. Can you make it?"

"I thought you didn't want me getting close to your family," she said softly.

"Naina, that was a misunderstanding. I didn't mean it like that," he said. "I'm sorry. Please, I really want you to come."

"Ok, I am not sure about the date. But I'll try and come," Naina said wondering if Abhay would go with her to the party.

"Great! It means a lot to me. See you at seven," he said and hung up.

Naina dialled Abhay's number and he picked up the phone and lowered the stereo volume. "Hi Naina. I wasn't expecting your call. I thought you would be busy with Aashiq. Oh sorry, Ashish."

Naina's face turned red at the mention of Ashish. "Abhay he was just here to see me as he was genuinely concerned about me. He ran back to Mumbai after meeting Constable Shukla. He isn't even taking my calls anymore."

Abhay covered the phone and laughed out, but controlled and said in a sullen tone, "Oh! That's so sad. Don't worry. *Main hoon na!*"

Naina slipped in her proposal. "Stop mocking that poor guy. Plus, I want your help. Uncle Chauhan has invited me to his home for dinner."

"Should I turn back towards their home? I am coming from there only."

"No! He has invited us *tomorrow* night! *Uff!*"

Abhay replied immediately, "I would love to go there and spread my love to dearest Girish and Suchitra Devi. I even want to get their fingerprints as they are prime suspects in my eyes."

Naina was dressed in a black sari, and a simple but elegant gold bracelet, necklace and earrings. She wanted to look her best to meet Uncle Chauhan's family. Tonight might be the night she unlocks the key to her past. And if it was, it would be her last night with Abhay. The case would be over, she would deal with the past, and she would move back to Mumbai. She had to do, what she had to. Naina retouched her makeup and brushed her hair one last time.

She heard loud music and the brakes of a car. She ran to the door and saw Abhay sitting in his jeep. Like a king on his throne. He was dressed in a black suit and white shirt. His red scarf made him look even more handsome.

Abhay was amazed to see Naina. His eyes lit up when he saw her.

And the jeep stereo continued: "*Dekha jo tujhe yaar, dil mein baji guitar…*"

"You look beautiful, Naina," he said.

"Thank you. You look quite handsome yourself," she said.

On the way to the party, Naina mentally prepared herself to meet Uncle Chauhan's family members. One of them could possibly be her parents' murderer and the thought that she was going to be at a party with the person deeply disturbed her. They soon reached the mansion. At the door, a maid greeted them and ushered them into the dining area.

Uncle Chauhan came over to Naina, his face aglow. "It's so nice to see you," he said wrapping her in a warm embrace.

All the doubts that Naina had about him vanished from her mind. Her uncle loved her. He could never do anything to hurt her. Abhay shook hands with Pradeep Chauhan when he finally let Naina go.

"It's nice to see you, Inspector Abhay Pandey," he said.

They walked into the luxurious dining room where the rest of the family was gathered. Naina's eye met with the formidable-looking Suchitra Devi Chauhan, who came and stood at the head of the table.

"Aagayi budhiya!" Abhay muttered in Naina's ears.

"Mother, you remember Naina?" Uncle Chauhan said.

"Yes I do. How are you, Naina?"

Naina forced a smile and ignored the sharp look the old woman gave them. "I'm fine, thank you."

"Would you like a drink?" Uncle Chauhan offered.

"Fresh lime will be fine." Naina wanted her wits about her tonight.

Tara came around and gave Naina a tight hug. "Hi, Naina. I'm so glad you could make it.

"Me too," Naina said, grateful to have a friend in the family.

Girish looked unshaven and quite drunk when he stumbled into the room. He slapped his father on the back, then hugged his grandmother.

Suchitra Devi winced. "Remember my sore arm, dear."

Abhay didn't fail to notice that Suchitra Devi's arm had suffered an injury. The older woman's wound was in the same place he thought Naina had stabbed her attacker.

Uncle Chauhan shot Girish a hard look. "It looks like you've been at it again, son." He wrinkled his nose. "Smells like it too."

"Girish, behave yourself!" Suchitra Devi admonished. "We have guests."

Everyone took their places for dinner.

"Bring Girish some fresh lime soda," Uncle Chauhan told the maid. "It will help him."

"No way. Get me a scotch," Girish said, his words slurring heavily.

The evening couldn't have been more uncomfortable. Naina picked at the fancy food and listened to Suchitra Devi Chauhan chatter about her social work. She made a futile attempt to ignore the foul smell of Girish's whiskey breath and his constant rude interruptions. Tara smiled at Naina across the table and helped ease some of the tension while Uncle Chauhan tried to change the topic of conversation to politics, primarily about Girish's campaign. Abhay wanted to punch everyone, it seemed.

"How's it going?" Abhay asked Girish.

"Who cares how it's going. Dad just wants somebody to carry on his legacy. That's why he adopted me. He's never considered me to be his own son. Are you going to—"

A collective gasp rose from the dining table.

"Girish! Stop blabbering nonsense," Uncle Chauhan lost control and shouted at him.

Seeing the situation go out of control, Suchitra Devi interrupted. "Enough of this for the moment. We can discuss this matter later."

Girish leaned forward on the table. "Well, Dad, are you going to tell everyone what this little dinner party is all about?"

Uncle Chauhan broke into a cough.

Girish gulped down another glass of scotch. "Oh, come on, Dad. I know why you invited Naina. You want us to get to know her."

Aur kitni jaan pehchaan badhaogey, jaan logey kya bachchi ki, Abhay thought.

"Well...that's right," Uncle Chauhan stuttered, his face turning red.

Tara Chauhan's spoon hit her plate with a thud. She frowned at Girish, "Daddy, you really should have never adopted him. He's an embarrassment to this family and not fit to be your heir."

Naina looked at Abhay and saw him studying the scene with an inspector's eye.

Girish stood up, making the table wobble. Silverware clinked and Tara caught her water glass just in time. Girish banged his fist on the table. "You guys are such fools. You're so caught up in your stupid politics and social work, you don't even see it."

"What are you talking about?" Tara looked shocked at her brother's outburst.

Uncle Chauhan reached for Girish's hand. "Let's talk in private."

"Shut up, Dad!" Girish yelled and shoved his father's hand away.

Suchitra Devi Chauhan gasped.

Girish steadied himself and glared at Naina. "I just found out that Dad's going to put her in his will!"

Chaos erupted in the room. Naina froze, too stunned to move as everyone stared at her.

"You can't do this!" Suchitra Devi Chauhan shouted.

"She's not a part of the family!" Girish yelled.

Tara's expression was unreadable as she watched her family fighting. It seemed as if she was already aware of these facts.

Seing all this confusion, Abhay slid away to get Suchitra Devi's and Girish's fingerprints.

"You little gold digger," Suchitra Devi said, pointing an accusing finger at Naina. "You came back to Allahabad to try and get money-"

"Mother, that's enough!" Uncle Chauhan yelled.

"Don't you talk to me in that tone, Pradeep Chauhan," Suchitra Devi snapped. "I'm your mother!"

The air in the room grew hot and heavy. Naina tugged at the neckline of her blouse, unable to breathe. Her head felt light and soon darkness descended around her, blocking out all the faces in the room. She closed her eyes so she wouldn't have to see the anger and fury as the people in the room fought and cursed. But she still heard their voices. The ugly names. The way it had happened many years back. The people talking about her as if she wasn't there, blaming her, telling her she wasn't a part of the family, arguing about her. Then, she saw the faint image of a man's face, etched with grief and anger. The man stretched his arms towards her, but his face was distorted, his hair hardly visible in the dim light. She could hear her mother's lullaby. The face moved closer, his eyes a grey mist in the glow of the bedroom lamp.

It was Uncle Chauhan.

Her mother screamed, her father cried out in agony. Uncle Chauhan was there. Blood dripped down her mother's stomach and collected in a pool on the floor. "No!" Naina screamed. She wrenched herself free from the memory and stared at the people around her. Her outburst silenced them all.

Naina's feet pounded the marble steps of the house into the night air. She flew across the lawn, panting and heaving for air. She had to escape. She had to get away from Uncle Chauhan. It had been him and she never once suspected him. She felt the cloud of betrayal breaking her heart. Suddenly someone's arms caught her, making her stop.

"Naina!" Abhay reached for her, but she pulled away and ran towards the gate. "Naina, wait!" he called out after her.

She fought him, thinking it was Uncle Chauhan.

"Stop running, Naina, it's me Abhay!"

His calm voice penetrated through her panic, and she stopped and fell limp in his arms.

"Let's get in the jeep. We'll talk there," he said.

When they were in the jeep and driving away, Abhay asked her. "You want to tell me what happened in there?"

Naina was quivering like a leaf in a storm. She took a deep breath. She'd come there to find out who her parents' killer was, and now she thought she knew. Only it was too hard to believe. Naina waited until the house disappeared from sight. Finally she closed her eyes, hoping the image would disappear too. She had to be wrong.

"Tell me what you saw," Abhay asked gently.

"Uncle Chauhan," Naina almost choked on the words.

"What do you mean...Uncle Chauhan?"

"He was there. At my parents' house the night they died." She stifled a sob. "I heard them arguing. My mother screaming. My dad. It was him." Naina covered her face with her hands, and Abhay pulled her to him.

"*Kya keh rahi ho Naina*? Uncle Chauhan was at your house a lot since he was friends with your parents. Could he have been there another night and you're confusing the nights?"

Naina shook her head. "I know what I saw. He was the vision in my dreams. Only this time I saw his face."

Abhay stroked her back. "I don't think he would have killed your parents."

"I only know what I saw," she said quietly.

"Maybe he showed up after the murder. I think it's someone else in the family," Abhay continued.

Naina nodded.

"Also, I managed to get Girish and Suchitra Devi Chauhan's fingerprints." Abhay said with a smile. "I'm going to drop them off at the lab later tonight." He glanced in the rear-view mirror for the first time. He'd been so worried about Naina that he hadn't noticed a black Mercedes with tinted black glasses on his tail. "Hold on. I think we're being followed."

She glanced back. Abhay swerved and sped up, turned onto a side road and took a U-turn. He wasn't the one to run. He headed back down the small road when the dark car came barrelling around the curve. Before they knew it, a gunshot exploded through the windshield.

Abhay groaned and grabbed his shoulder as a bullet pierced his shoulder. He'd been hit. Naina screamed. Abhay tried to steer the car, but a stream of blood flowed from his shoulder, and his vision became blurry. The gun fired again, but Abhay continued driving. Feeling dizzy, he blinked and reached for Naina. She ripped off the end of her sari and tied it to his shoulder to stop the bleeding. He felt weak and lightheaded.

Naina realized that Abhay couldn't continue for too long in this state. "Pull over. I'll drive," Naina said, taking control.

Abhay didn't want to lose his control. He could handle a bullet. But Naina begged him to stop.

He stopped the car and crawled to the passenger side. She drove like the wind to the nearest hospital. She jumped out at the emergency room entry and shouted, "A man's been shot! Someone help me!" A doctor and a few nurses rushed to her aid. They eased Abhay onto a stretcher and wheeled him into the operation theatre, firmly pushing Naina aside. Abhay looked at the nurse – the same long-legged nurse he had earlier met. Finally he was in bed with her. Not like he had envisaged. But Still.

An hour later, the doctor returned. "He's lost some blood and he's weak, but he'll be fine now that the bullet has been extracted," he said.

The doctor looked at her blood-soaked clothes and asked. "Are you alright? Did you hurt yourself?"

"No. I think the bullet was meant for me, but it missed. Can I meet him, doctor?"

"Not right now, but I will let you know when the time is right." The doctor went away, leaving Naina with her thoughts.

She glanced down at her blood-soaked clothes, then closed her eyes and whispered another prayer. It was her fault that Abhay was hurt. All she did was bring trouble into people's lives. She had to get away from him. As she prayed, Abhay's image blurred, and instead of his handsome face, she saw her parents lying on the floor of her house, saw another shadow hovering in the corner. She needed to remember the whole night of her parents' death. Uncle Chauhan had been there, but there had been another shadow, another person that she couldn't remember. She had to know who it was. She slipped out of the hospital and went back to her house to see if she could remember the rest of the story. Then she could say goodbye to her past and Abhay. For his own safety.

Abhay struggled to open his eyes, but they felt as if they'd been pressed down by boulders. And the rest of his body felt worse. What the hell had happened?

Then he remembered. The fight at the Chauhan mansion. Naina's memory. The car following them. The bullet.

He groaned and tried to raise his arm, but one side was taped with a bandage, the other secured with an IV. *Damn.* He couldn't move. Then the green walls of the hospital room started closing in on him.

He couldn't just lie here. Not when Naina was in danger. Where was she, anyway?

He made a feeble attempt to call for help, but his words came out garbled, and his eyes were so heavy he couldn't keep them open.

Medication. He must still be on the anaesthetic. God, he needed to wake up. He swung his arms and legs, but nothing happened and he realized the drugs were so strong that it was difficult to fight their effects. Heaviness weighed him down.

The minute she opened the door, Naina knew tonight was going to be different. It was already past midnight, and darkness had enveloped her house, so she switched on the lights. But there seemed to be a power cut. She groped her way to her parents' bedroom, where it had all happened.

Snatches of memories flashed through her mind – her mother's lullaby and her father's deep voice calling her name. She heard a sound in the living room. She stopped for a moment and strained her ears. Nothing. She'd probably imagined it.

She passed by her room and knelt beside the place on the floor where her parents had died. Just then, she heard another sound. A faint scraping of steps. A chill went up her spine as a shadow formed behind Naina.

Was it real or a shadow from her memory?

The shadow, framed in the doorway, slowly turned, and squinted in the heavy darkness.

"It was you," Naina said softly, recognizing the shadow, the one from her nightmare. Except this time, it was real.

Abhay pushed the doctor away and snatched out the IV, wincing in pain.

Uncle Chauhan rushed. "Where's Naina? Was she hurt? I came as soon as I heard."

Abhay saw the worry lines on Uncle Chauhan's face. Naina had suspected him, but he still couldn't believe her Uncle would hurt her. "I am not sure where Naina is, though I have a hunch." Abhay snapped. "And if I get out of this god-damned hospital, I am sure I can find her."

"You've just had a surgery, young man. You're not going anywhere." The doctor folded his arms and blocked the way.

Abhay snarled. "I do what I feel like. When I feel like. And never forget that!"

The doctor stepped back seeing the daroga seething in anger.

Abhay dressed quickly, and Uncle Chauhan slid his shoulder under Abhay's arm to give him support. When they were in the jeep, Uncle Chauhan looked at Abhay for directions.

"If you want Naina to be safe, then take me to her house this minute," Abhay said. "I have to save Naina."

Uncle Chauhan stepped on the accelerator. "Abhay, you really care about Naina, don't you?" he finally said.

"Yes, I care about every case that I need to solve. *Koi shak?*"

"Then that gives us something in common."

"But do *you* care about her?" Abhay asked, wincing in pain.

"Yes, I do," Uncle Chauhan said quietly. "I love her very much. And I have to tell you something. I should have made this public years ago...but I was a coward. The truth is, Abhay, Naina is my daughter."

A torrent of scattered, painful moments came crashing back to Naina. The realization was too much of a shock for her.

"Tara, it was you! You were here that night. But why?"

The woman Naina had thought was her friend walked into the room, her body as sleek and cunning as a leopard. When she spoke, her voice was wild and razor sharp. "You knew it all the time. You never lost your memory. You played this stupid game so you could come back and get daddy's money."

"What are you talking about, Tara?"

Tara's eyes blazed with hatred and she waved a knife in front of her.

A cold feeling crept over Naina. Yes, she had seen it before. Those eyes. She'd seen that crazy look on Tara's face the night her parents had died.

"You wanted Daddy's money," Tara hissed. "You came back to destroy our family. You wanted to take him away from me, just like you would have years ago." She paced the room, the knife gripped tightly in her hand.

"That's not true," Naina said.

"But you're not part of our family. And you will *never be*!" Tara yelled, kicking the end table and sending the lamp crashing to the floor. It shattered into pieces at Naina's feet. "I was Daddy's little girl. All he thought of was you or about having a son who could follow his footsteps and be a minister like him. So he adopted that useless Girish! It was bad enough that I had to share Daddy with you and then that Girish came along and he thought *he* was Daddy's favourite. But he wasn't. I am using his car tonight and I have his fingerprints on this knife. After I kill you, and he too is wiped out from my life, I will be Daddy's girl once again."

Naina froze, afraid to say anything that might make Tara angrier.

"I was Daddy's favourite. I should have all his money. Not Girish. And definitely not you…his illegitimate child!"

"I know I'm not part of your family," Naina said, fighting her own emotions. "I never–"

"Shut up!" Tara screamed. "You were there that night when daddy came to ask for you."

"Tara, I don't know what you are talking about," she lied. It was all coming back to her. The fight between her parents had started when Uncle Chauhan burst in.

Pradeep Chauhan was her father. A shudder racked through her at the realization. That was the reason her parents had fought.

Her father was crying. "What do you mean she's not my baby?" He asked in disbelief.

Her mother said through sobs, "I was pregnant when we got married."

"With my baby!" Uncle Chauhan yelled. He then yelled at her mother. "Why didn't you tell me you were pregnant?"

"Because you were running for elections. And your mother threatened me. She warned me that if I didn't keep this to myself, I would ruin your career and my life."

"I don't believe that," Uncle Chauhan shouted.

Her father stood quietly in disbelief. Naina watched all of it from her hiding place. She watched her family fall apart. Her father had accused her mother of lying to him. Her mother had cried till she couldn't talk. Uncle Chauhan had been furious. He had said he'd just found out the truth and wanted to claim Naina as his own. Her mother had yelled that he would never get her. Her father had threatened to leave her mother. Then Uncle Chauhan had stormed out.

But her parents had still been alive when he had left.

She looked at Tara, and the memory of her sneaking into the house came back vividly.

Tara had been young and beautiful, but the evil she'd possessed had caused her to attack Naina's mother. She had run in, yelling that she wanted to see Naina. In a wild rage, Tara managed to grab the kitchen knife and fought with her mother. Her mother had been trying to protect Naina, to keep Tara from finding her. Then Tara stabbed her mother, and her mother had fallen to the floor with a scream. Her father had rushed in, and Tara had spun around and lunged at him with the knife. Even as a child, she'd been amazed at Tara's strength. Tara, all wild-eyed, had come looking for her but she couldn't find her as she couldn't be in the house *for very long or her crime might be discovered. All the while, Naina had hidden under the bed and watched, holding her breath, knowing she was going to be next.*

Just like now.

"Tara, I didn't remember," Naina said. "All this time, I didn't know."

"Liar! You didn't know he was your father?" Tara spat the words at her and held the knife to her neck. "Well, you remember now. I can see it on your face. When Daddy first learned that you had come back to Allahabad, that's when he changed his will to include you. Don't tell me you didn't know that, you greedy bitch!"

"But...but I didn't," Naina stammered.

"Then he started inviting you over, wanting us to get to know you. I knew the truth and I hated you."

Tears streaked down Naina's face. The situation was slipping out of control, but she knew that she had to distract Tara a little longer, to try to talk some sense into her. "So you shot Abhay."

"That bullet was meant for you. Just like the knife."

"And it was you who broke into my house and tried to kill me."

"Of course. All it took was a little help from my friend Ria."

She flashed an evil smirk and continued, "Do you remember the lovely tea that Ria always made for you? Well, she was drugging it all along."

It dawned on Naina – how easy it had been for Tara. "So Ria was helping you? But why, for money?"

Tara laughed, "Obviously. Such people have no principles in life. They would sell their soul for pennies. I even hired a goon to assassinate you, but he failed, and

I had to get him killed. The bastard died in a pool of piss, which he rightly deserved."

All made perfect sense now. "And she had my keys…."

Tara looked triumphant. "It was a great plan. I thought we'd succeed in making you go nuts before I had to kill you. But you're stronger than I thought."

Naina was too shocked to react, and Tara too indifferent to her fear. "When Ria drugged your tea at the office before our lunch, I was hoping you'd fall asleep in your car and have an accident."

"But I showed up for our lunch meeting and got sick."

"Right," Tara pressed the knife into Naina's neck, laughing.

"And the brooch?

"Oh, that was just to confuse Abhay. To make him believe that you were crazy." Tara narrowed her eyes. "And now…you're going to die just like your parents."

Naina took a deep breath. Everyone had thought that she was the crazy one, when Tara had obviously been unstable all her life. She was not going to let Tara kill her. She was not going to die before seeing Tara rot in jail or a mental ward. Tara licked her lips like a predator coming in for the kill, and Naina knew the time had come to defend herself.

"Hurry!" Abhay bellowed as Uncle Chauhan sped down the road. The traffic lights glowed an angry red in the darkness but Pradeep Chauhan ignored them, speeding the car straight to Naina's home.

"Are you sure she'll be there?"

"No, but it's my best guess. She would have gone there to try and regain her memory."

When they turned the corner to Naina's house, they spotted a black Mercedes parked in front of her house.

"Girish's car?" Uncle chauhan said. "What the hell… Is he the one trying to kill Naina?"

Abhay didn't think so, but he didn't tell the old man that. As they got out of the car, Abhay called in for backup. They padded up to the door and Abhay put a finger to his lips. Just as they made the last step, Abhay heard a scream.

He bolted through the door, sending a fresh wave of pain jolting through his shoulder. He'd probably undone his stitches, but he didn't care. He never did.

He raced through the living room toward Naina's parents' room. Uncle Chauhan hurried behind him.

Naina was struggling with Tara. Their heavy breathing and scuffling filled the air. Tara pushed Naina down to the floor with a kick to her stomach and climbed over her, lowering the knife to Naina's neck.

"Tara, stop!" Uncle Chauhan shouted.

Tara turned to see her father and Abhay rushing towards her. Abhay took the opportunity to grab Tara's arm. Tara struggled, clawing at him. Naina took her chance and slipped out from under Tara. Abhay managed to lock both of Tara's hands behind her and pried the knife from her fingers. Tara glared at him with fury. She kicked and screamed. "She has to die! She has to!"

Abhay pulled her aside and gave her one tidy slap on her face.

"Agar bachpan mein tumhare pita ney aisa jhaapad mara hota, toh aaj yeh din na dekhna padta."

Abhay turned towards Chauhan and continued. "Mr Chauhan, your daughter Tara murdered Naina's parents and assaulted Naina," he showed them the injury on Tara's arm that Naina had inflicted. "She's going to be charged and she will rot in jail. Had you not been busy in your shit politics and been a bit more responsible towards your family, you could have saved two lives."

"Tara, my God, what have you done..." Uncle Chauhan said, choking on his words, and falling to his knees.

Shuklaji peeped in from the main door with backup.

"*Badi jaldi aa gaye aap Shuklaji,*" Abhay said sarcastically.

"*Sirji, woh baat nahin hain na.* I actually tried my best, I promise, but still couldn't reach sirji," Shukla said as he motioned the team to take Tara into custody.

Tara was taken into custody. Her frantic, hysterical sobs had died, and she looked like a shattered, injured animal.

Uncle Chauhan went to Naina and wrapped his arms around her. "I know I made some terrible mistakes, Naina, but I hope you will forgive me one day. I didn't know your mother was pregnant when I broke up with her. I was young and ambitious and foolish. I had no idea."

"And you didn't know your mother threatened her?"

"No. I was caught up in the campaign. Back then, I allowed my mother to run my life. But when I found out about you..." he paused and squeezed her hand, "I was so afraid you'd hate me."

The sincerity in his voice tugged at Naina's heart.

"Please don't hate me. I'd like to see you again, Naina," Uncle Chauhan said.

Naina hesitated. "So do I, but please give me some time."

He bent down and kissed her forehead. "I'll be waiting, my child."

Naina ran to Abhay and pulled him to her. She ran her hands over his body to check for injuries. Naina clung to him, her breath erratic. She felt her heart pounding as she hugged him.

"Are you hurt?"

"I'm okay," Abhay whispered.

He spotted blood on her blouse and said, "But you're bleeding."

A soft nervous laugh escaped Naina. "It's not me. It's you. I think your stitches have come undone."

Abhay looked down and realized blood was seeping through his bandage. His shoulder and arm throbbed.

Naina looked up at him, her eyes brimming with tears. She said, "Abhay, how can I ever thank you for all that you've done…"

Ek pappi dekar, he thought.

She continued, "This has been the darkest hour of my life and now I'm going to make it worse… I've come to a decision; I'm going to move back to Mumbai. This town has too many ghosts from my past. I want a new life, a fresh start. As much as I want to stay here with you…I've realized that I can't…'

Yeh toh hona hee tha, he thought.

"We can decide the future later. What matters for now is that I have you safe in my arms."

Shukla entered, "Sirji, actually today is a big victory, so I have asked the team to arrange a decent victory party. If you know what I mean sirji." He giggled.

Inspector Abhay Pandey knew how decent their victory parties were. He smirked at Shukla's honesty.

"Kya baat kartey ho Shuklaji, let's go! Rani Mera intezaar kar rahi hogi."

www.ingramcontent.com/pod-product-compliance
Lightning Source LLC
Chambersburg PA
CBHW071927220626
47052CB00002B/497